"Where's the *male* courier?"

At her puzzled glance, he continued briskly. "The male courier who's accompanying you."

"There isn't one."

"I was told there was a D. Tredinnick."

"I'm Dee Tredinnick. *D-e-e*." Dee spelled it out with some satisfaction. Clearly this man didn't think a mere woman was capable of working as a courier.

"You don't mean—you can't mean—that a girl has been sent here alone on such a mission?" His surprise and anger were as obvious as they were insulting.

With an effort, she strove to speak calmly. "I assure you, Mr. Ransom—"

He swept aside her words as if she hadn't spoken. "Nothing about this business reassures me. Is your boss aware that you'll be turned loose on Delhi, alone?"

The man was impossible! "Delhi is in no danger from me," Dee shot back through gritted teeth. "I don't bite."

Sue Peters grew up in the idyllic countryside of Warwickshire, England, and began writing romance novels quite by chance. "Have a go," her mother suggested when a national writing contest sponsored by Mills & Boon appeared in the local newspaper. Sue's entry placed second, and a career was born.

Books by Sue Peters

HARLEQUIN ROMANCE

MAID FOR MARRIAGE
Sue Peters

Harlequin Books

TORONTO • NEW YORK • LONDON
AMSTERDAM • PARIS • SYDNEY • HAMBURG
STOCKHOLM • ATHENS • TOKYO • MILAN
MADRID • WARSAW • BUDAPEST • AUCKLAND

ISBN 0-373-17159-5

MAID FOR MARRIAGE

'THREE times a bridesmaid. You want to watch it, young Dee,' Oliver teased, and tweaked a lock of shiny dark hair which had managed to escape from under the restricting halo of artificial flowers that adorned his sister's neat head. 'You know what they say about never being a bride.'

'Don't *you* harp,' Dee groaned. 'I've heard all I want to on that subject from Mother. And if you upset this head-dress I shall get into even more trouble with her. She took over half an hour to fix the wretched thing to her liking.'

Hastily Dee ducked away from her brother's reach, putting up one hand to steady the head-dress. Her sudden movement imperilled the slice of wedding cake which she held in the other, precariously balanced on a scarcely adequate plate.

'I wonder if I can manage to smuggle this out to Scruffy,' she wondered out loud. 'He'd enjoy all the sticky marzipan and icing.'

'That's typical of you,' Oliver's wife laughed, safe in the occupation of one of the few seats in the crowded marquee, hers by right of her interesting condition. 'You don't give good wedding cake to a dog,' she scolded. 'You either eat it, or put it under your pillow so you'll dream of your husband-to-be.'

'Did you dream about Oliver before you were married?'

'I didn't need to. We'd been dreaming about one another ever since we were at school together.'

Dee hid a grimace. So cut and dried. Predictable to the point of boredom. Just like her second sister's marriage this morning, and her older sister's wedding two years previously. She cast a glance to where the new bridegroom was shaking hands with some late-arriving guests, and no doubt saying all the right things.

He was nice enough. So were the others. But totally unexciting. At twenty-three, Dee had no intention of mortgaging the rest of her life for the doubtful privilege of wearing a wedding-ring.

A year ago she had thought just the opposite. That was before she had found out about Alan. She stirred restlessly, and decided, trying not to sound bitter, 'I'll eat my cake myself. I can use being three times a bridesmaid as an insurance policy.'

Her sister-in-law's look struggled between amusement and exasperation. 'I never knew anyone so reluctant to fall in love.'

Her family did not know about Alan. Dee said defensively, 'There's nothing wrong with wanting to stay solo.'

'That seems to be your theme song. Love won't wait for you forever. You'll end up being an old maid. You'll sit on the shelf, and be taken down and dusted every other bank holiday. Doesn't the thought appal you?'

'No.' Dee's denial was muffled by marzipan, but the emphatic shake of her head made up for any lack of clarity.

Exasperation won, and the older woman scolded, 'Never has a girl passed by so many opportunities. You've been brought up in a university town absolutely crammed full of students of all shapes and sizes, all of them high fliers. Surely one of them must have had some appeal for you, somewhere along the line? You get invited to every function that's going, and then some, and it isn't just because your father's a senior don either.'

'To say nothing of having a mother who's the town's most active matchmaker,' Oliver put in wickedly. His sister's huge dark eyes, which could melt or sparkle at their owner's whim, had more than a little to do with the invitations, he reflected as his wife went on,

'Hasn't one of them made any impression on you?'

'Mmm.'

It could have meant yes, or it could have meant no, and the last bit of icing and marzipan made the perfect excuse for Dee not to enlarge.

Alan was not a student, but the impression he had made was both lasting and painful. He was Dee's first serious love, but she had learned the hard way that she was not his.

Alan was the architect who had come to advise on the restoration of the stone work of one of the colleges, and from the moment he had espied Dee walking home across the grounds he had pursued her.

Since she was more accustomed to the company of students in her own age group, Alan's attentions had at first flattered her, and then swept her off her feet with his glib tongue and apparent sophistication, against which her own naïveté had given her no defence.

Until the evening in the chic restaurant, when Alan's wife had arrived at the same time as the coffee and liqueurs. The lady had been furious, vocal, and heavily pregnant, and Dee still cringed at the memory of the scene which had followed.

Shocked and bewildered, she had turned on Alan. 'You told me——'

'I didn't say anything about marriage,' he had countered quickly, and, with hindsight, Dee realised he'd spoken the truth, for once. Alan's promises were as insubstantial as his lifestyle, and marriage had simply been an assumption on her part, which she now knew to be incredibly naïve.

Her only consolation had to be that the restaurant was a long way out of town, and there had been no one there that she knew to witness her humiliation, or to bring back news of the sordid affair to the ears of her family.

It was a long time before Dee had felt able to look the world in the face again after that evening. Now at last she could, and she knew exactly what it was she wanted from it.

Her plans did not include men. She felt as if she would never trust another man, for as long as she lived. In future, she decided, she would remain her own woman, and confine her ambitions to seeing as much of the world as possible.

Ambition was a safer bet than love. It could not hurt. And the world would always be there, it would not disappear in a flurry of weak excuses, as had Alan, and leave her to pick up the pieces as best she might.

A timely opening with a local firm had made an excellent springboard for her ambition to travel, and if her new boss felt surprise at the force of her declaration that she was free from male commitments, either present or in the future, her determined, 'I want to travel. And I can't pack a husband into a suitcase,' had satisfied him sufficiently to offer her the job.

'Your insurance policy won't work,' Oliver predicted now. 'With me safely married, and Jane and Felicity off her hands, Mother won't have anyone else but you to turn her talents to. What's the betting that this time next year you'll be eating your own wedding cake?'

'No chance.' Dee stabbed at the remaining crumbs on her plate with a positive forefinger, and licked off the results. 'You'll lose your bet. I'm a confirmed bachelor girl. By the time Mother's recovered from organising this lot,' she waved her now empty plate in the direction of the smartly dressed assembly crowded into the huge marquee, 'I'll be safely out of her reach, in India.'

'You might escape your mother, but don't imagine you can escape Cupid,' her sister-in-law warned. 'With your looks he'll catch up with you yet.'

'He won't if I travel fast enough, and far enough.'

Her job as a courier with WW enabled her to do both. The initials stood for William Williams, or Bill, as their boss was familiarly known to all his staff. The letters also stood for world-wide. It was Bill's proud boast that he could despatch or collect any item to or from any part of the globe at a moment's notice, personally escorted by a member of his staff, so that clients anxiously awaiting some precious consignment could rest assured that it would be delivered safely into their hands by a courier already known to them.

The service was not cheap. WW only dealt in upmarket valuables, but such was the firm's reputation that they were never at a loss for work. World-famous jewellers, silversmiths, and dealers in priceless antiques and equally precious artefacts of all kinds, including paintings, beat a path to their door.

Under pressure from their satisfied clients, WW expanded operations to include organising exhibitions of the precious wares they handled and it was to collect items for one such function that Dee was due in India at the weekend.

It was to be her first long-haul trip. Up until now her journeys on the firm's behalf had been confined more or less to the continent, Italy being her furthest destination. She could hardly believe her luck when Bill had called her into his office one morning, several weeks previously, and announced without preamble, 'By the time you get back from your next trip I'll have the papers processed for you to go to Delhi.'

'Delhi?' Dee gasped, unable to hide her delight.

'Delhi,' Bill confirmed. 'It's time you began to spread your wings a bit.'

It was his way of telling her that he was more than satisfied with the way she had conducted her work so far, and Dee received the accolade with a pleased nod, and an interested, 'What's the trip in aid of?'

'We've been asked to stage an exhibition on the theme of craft-work through the ages. The guilds are sponsoring it, and it will be mostly jewellery, silverware and ceramics.'

'Only from India?'

'No, the exhibits will be coming from all over the world. We'll be collecting from Egypt, India,

Japan, Russia—you name it. And, of course, the continent as well, but the team that's in Paris next week can disperse to cover that. You'll be collecting the Indian exhibits from our contact in Delhi.'

'Will they be big or heavy?' The size and weight would affect how the consignment was crated, and whether it would travel by air or by sea, which in turn would dictate what luggage Dee would need to pack for her own personal use.

'They shouldn't be, although our contact over there will have the final choice of what to send, but I'm told it will be jewellery for the most part, and small items, so you'll be able to travel by air. I'm told some of the pieces once belonged to a maharajah, so don't drop them,' he teased.

'I wouldn't dream of it,' Dee promised gleefully, and added, 'Where are you staging the exhibition?'

'In the UK, but I haven't decided on exactly where yet. I'll keep the exhibits in our vaults here if necessary until that part has been sorted out. The National Exhibition Centre, just outside Birmingham, was one suggestion.'

'But not coming from you?' Dee sensed Bill's reservations, although he had used the venue on many occasions before and was enthusiastic about the excellent facilities it offered.

'It's ideal for most jobs, but not this one. For one thing, we shan't need so much space. The exhibition won't be open to the general public.

Entry will be by invitation only, which is why having a fairly short notice of the venue won't matter.'

'It sounds as if there might be more exhibits than visitors.'

'With a collection of items of this value access will have to be restricted, for security's sake. It's aimed at upmarket, specialist people only, with one or two of the wealthier private collectors allowed in for good measure. For this reason alone I'd like to stage it in a setting that will show off the exhibits to their best advantage.'

'Like Windsor Castle, for example?' Dee grinned.

'Windsor Castle would do at a pinch,' her boss conceded, and removed her grin with, 'Go and see the company medic about getting your jabs started. You'll need about four on my reckoning, and they'll all hurt.'

The pain and the subsequent malaise were worth it. India exploded on Dee's consciousness with all the colour of a splintered rainbow. Bill's contact met her at Delhi airport.

'Did you have a good flight?' he enquired as he rescued her luggage and steered her through a clamour of local entrepreneurs, all eager to purchase her non-existent duty frees.

Her smiling head-shake convinced them of her lack, and they transferred their attentions to other, more likely passengers, and Dee followed her guide to the car which he had parked in readiness. He helped her into the passenger-seat, and disposed of her luggage in the back before adding, 'Would you like a meal, or have you eaten?'

'The flight was fine, and I ate on the plane, thanks. Although a cup of tea would be welcome.'

'In that case, we'll head straight for your hotel. We can talk after you've settled in.'

There was scant opportunity for conversation on the way. With the promise, 'I'll take a short cut through the back streets; they're a bit crowded, but it will be quicker in the long run than going all the way round,' her companion keyed the engine into life, and sent the car hurtling at speed to join the nightmare mixture of humanity on the move that was Delhi traffic, and which made Dee thankful that it was not she who was at the wheel.

Even Paris traffic could not compare with this, she decided, awed. No boulevard could possibly produce the mixture of auto-rickshaws, camel carts, loaded donkeys, and equally loaded motor-scooters. Some of the latter carried as many as four adults, she counted in amazement, and stared in disbelief at a miniature motor vehicle, which had been designed to carry only one person, and which had almost disappeared under its outrageous load.

Immediately that the car turned off the main thoroughfare into a side-street a seeming impenetrable mass of people confronted them, intermingled with animals of every conceivable size and description.

'You'll have to turn back,' Dee gasped. 'You'll never get through a scrum like this.'

'Why not?' her driver enquired laconically and carried blithely on, with one foot pressed down hard on the accelerator, and one hand pressed equally hard on the horn.

His ploy worked, but the din was deafening. Dee winced as shouts from street bazaar traders vied with motor horns for attention, while she marvelled at the cool nerve of the man at the wheel.

'Look out!' she cried as a child darted inches in front of their bonnet.

Her companion swung his wheel, missing the boy by a hair's breadth, and made Dee grab for anchorage when he immediately swung it back again to avoid an ambling cow heading with hungry intent towards a display of fruit and vegetables piled on the nearby pavement.

Dee longed to close her eyes, but brilliant colour dazzled her senses, keeping her lids wide with wonder.

Bright turbans, intricately wound, made vivid splashes among the more delicately shaded saris which fluttered in the breeze like colourful butterflies as their wearers bargained briskly with the street traders, seemingly impervious to the dust and the heat that beat down upon them. Bill had apologised in advance about the heat.

'Sorry the cooler weather's a week or two away, but the heat shouldn't be unbearable. The thermometer hasn't reached the bottom line yet, but it's beginning to head downwards.'

'I can cope. I don't mind heat,' Dee had declared with the confidence of the uninitiated. 'Anyway, I shan't be there for more than a night or two. As soon as I've met up with our contact over there I can book the next available flight back.'

The look Bill had thrown at her had held a trace of irony, but he'd said nothing more, although Dee had noticed that her flight tickets were open-ended, the return date being left for negotiation.

This was not unusual, however, such being the nature of her journeys for the firm, and it had excited no questions in her mind. Bill had sufficient trust in his couriers to allow them some flexibility.

An intersection of the side-streets brought them to a temporary halt beside a spice vendor's stall, and aromatic air wafted tantalisingly through the open window.

Dee's appreciative, 'Mm, lovely,' turned to a disgusted, 'Ugh!' as she frantically wound up the window against the blast of exhaust fumes that started the traffic moving again, and a few minutes later the side-street ejected them on to a wide tree-lined thoroughfare that was in total contrast to the crowded, narrow alleyways they had left behind.

So, too, was the imposing hotel, set in its own gardens, before which her companion eventually pulled to a halt, with the remark, 'You should be comfortable here.'

He was given to understatement, Dee reflected, surveying her luxurious *en suite* accommodation, but she had no time now in which to relax and enjoy it. Her contact was due to return in under an hour and take her to see the exhibits she had come to India to collect.

Refreshed by a shower, a change of clothes, and the tray of tea which had been thoughtfully sent to her room, she was waiting in the foyer when her escort called back.

'It isn't far, and it's main road all the way this time,' he promised, and was as good as his word when, less than twenty minutes later, he ushered Dee into the cool entrance hall of an official-looking building which she supposed to be a bank.

Her guess proved correct, and the vaults mounted guard over the precious artefacts an indication, if she needed one, of what their value must be.

'They're beautiful!' she exclaimed as she surveyed the items laid out on a black velvet cloth for her inspection, and marvelled at the imaginative artistry that had gone into their composition.

'What must it feel like to be rich enough to own such lovely things?' she wondered wistfully, and her companion's tone was dry as he answered, with truth,

'You and I are unlikely ever to know.'

A delicate pendant, inlaid with precious stones, and each gem itself beautifully engraved, was flanked on the one side by a miniature painting of exquisite beauty, set in a jewel-encrusted mount.

On its other side lay a collection of necklaces, ear pendants, rings, and bangles for both ankle and wrist, all lying in glittering splendour, fashioned in gold and silver, and set with jewels worth a king's ransom.

'We'll provide you with an escort for your journey back to London, of course,' her companion said matter-of-factly, and Dee nodded.

Some clients provided their own escort, depending upon the value of the consignment. Some did not, preferring to rely upon heavy insurance cover if anything went wrong.

The priceless collection twinkling up at her from the black velvet drape made Dee thankful that their client had chosen the former course on this particular occasion, not because she doubted her own competence, but because Bill's training had made her well aware of the vulnerability of a sole courier carrying a priceless collection of gems. Having a companion would halve the very real risk. She dragged her eyes away from the dazzling display as her companion spoke again.

'There are still a number of pieces to come, to complete the exhibit.' He carefully folded the black velvet over the glittering fire, and transferred the precious parcel to a safe deposit box. 'As soon as they arrive I'll have the necessary documentation filled in, ready for their transfer to London.'

'Let me know when you receive them,' Dee replied. 'That way I can book the first available return flight. I'll remain in my room at the hotel tomorrow until I hear from you.'

Her companion looked taken aback. 'There will be no need for you to do that. It would be a pity for you to miss the sights, now you are here.'

Dee felt she would very much like to see the sights, but she was not here on a sightseeing trip. Bill trusted his couriers not to waste time on their travels, and she had no intention of betraying that trust. She answered firmly, 'If I happen to be out when you ring it might mean that I'll miss the chance of a seat on a London flight tomorrow.'

The darkly handsome face on the opposite side of the table broke into a smile. 'You won't be going back for a day or two, at the very least. You'll have plenty of time to get acquainted with Delhi. Even if the rest of the exhibits arrive quickly——' his tone questioned that possibility

'—your escort won't be ready to leave until Thursday at the earliest.'

Today was Saturday. Dee made a rapid count. 'That's another five whole days,' she protested, and felt thankful that Bill had not yet settled on a venue for the exhibition. If he had, her own particular consignment would have looked likely to be the one exhibit missing. 'Surely whoever my escort is can...' she began, and her companion shook his head.

'He's Luke Ransom. You may already know him.'

'Do you mean Luke Ransom the antiques dealer?' A nod confirmed her guess, and Dee added, 'I don't know him personally. I've heard of him, of course.'

Who had not? In the world of the rare, and the beautiful, Luke Ransom was king. His sphere was far removed from that of the collectors' mass market. The treasures which passed through his hands were one-offs, of fabulous worth, meant for discerning collectors of equally fabulous wealth. He did not use WW for conveying his treasures. Luke Ransom was the sort of man who relied upon no one but himself.

He was known as an authority on silver and porcelain, and travelled the world in search of pieces to bring back to his small and exclusive bow-fronted shop in one of the most select districts of London.

Dee had passed it once, on her way back from visiting one of Bill's clients, and curiosity had made her pause to gaze in at the window. There had been little to see, but lack of quantity had been more than compensated for by quality.

A single porcelain vase, of goodness knew what antiquity, had rested on a length of wild silk which had been draped with seeming carelessness across the back of the window, but which never-theless had managed to pick out exactly the main colours of the porcelain and highlighted its fragile beauty to perfection.

Nothing so vulgar as a price tag showed itself in Luke Ransom's window, and Dee had hurried on her way, musing as to the kind of wealth that could purchase such a treasure.

Perhaps, in the end, the antiques dealer might decide to keep it for himself? Maybe he was one of those avid collectors who could not bear to part with his artefacts? With his sort of ex-pertise, doubtless built up over a long lifetime of experience, he was probably a bit of an antique himself, she'd reflected.

Although within the trade Luke Ransom's name was one to conjure with, Dee had never actually set eyes on him, or even seen a photo-graph of him in the newspapers. He had the reputation of being a very private individual, who shunned publicity, and, since the work of Bill's couriers was finished when they delivered their particular consignment into the hands of the client, and they did not themselves attend any of the actual exhibitions, only their own clients became known to them personally.

It would be interesting to meet the famous antiques dealer, Dee thought, and hid a smile at the prospect of his acting as her escort. If he was as antique himself as she suspected he would be more of a liability than an asset, from a security angle.

She persisted, 'Can't he possibly make it earlier than Thursday? If the exhibits arrive before then, I mean?' A possibility struck her. 'If he isn't in the country yet I'm quite prepared to take them back on my own.'

'Mr Ransom has been in India for some days. He's on his way back from Japan. I believe he has been over there, negotiating for some particularly fine pieces of porcelain for a special client. He broke his journey in Delhi in order to visit an old school friend.'

'*Old* school friend' fitted in with Dee's guesstimate as to Luke Ransom's possible age. With an effort she curbed her growing impatience, and insisted, 'In that case, surely he could be ready to fly out as soon as you have all the exhibits together and the documentation ready?'

'Oh, no.' Her companion's tone became almost reverent. 'Nothing would induce Mr Ransom to go before Thursday. He'll be at the cricket match on Wednesday.'

'Cricket match?' Dee wondered if she had heard aright. She took in a deep breath, and repeated carefully, 'Cricket match?'

'That's right. It's a big charity match, with all the top players taking part.' The reverence was obvious now, and confirmed the speaker, too, as a devotee of the game.

Dee let out her breath in a carefully measured hiss. Luke Ransom was evidently one of those crusty, arrogant old Colonel Blimp kind of creatures who expected the entire world to grind to a halt merely because he wanted to see, of all things, a game of cricket.

In vain she tried to persuade her companion to allow her to go alone, but he was not to be deflected from his purpose. Mr Ransom had been approached on the subject of providing an escort, and he had agreed to take on the task himself, in view of the priceless nature of the exhibits.

But not before Thursday.

'Have a look round the city. Enjoy the sights while you can,' Dee was urged.

With difficulty she forbore to point out that the sight she most wanted to see was the aforesaid Mr Ransom, plus herself carrying the exhibits, boarding a plane bound for London.

There was nothing to be gained by further argument, however, and with a guilty feeling of committing severe dereliction of duty Dee acted upon her companion's advice the following morning and set out with a guidebook, provided by the hotel, to obtain her first glimpse of Delhi.

Frustration at the delay, mingled with the knowledge that it might be a long time before another such opportunity presented itself, drove Dee to more activity than was strictly wise until she had become accustomed to the humid end-of-monsoon heat, but it had an advantage in that there were, as yet, fewer tourists to add to the already formidable congestion in the narrow streets of the old city.

She visited temples and mosques, turned her back on the impressive legacy left by Lutyens and Baker in the new part of the city, and dived happily into the narrow, packed streets through which she had been driven the day before, fascinated alike by the throbbing, noisy life of the bazaars, and the intricately carved buildings which bore images of people and animals from another era, frozen in stone on the walls, and gazing down impassively from their elevated stance upon the teeming modern life below them.

She purchased a dazzling silk headscarf to protect herself from the sun—and lost it to the clutching paws of a daring troupe of monkeys clambering about an ancient fort—and returned, drained by the heat and the exertions of the day, to the welcome coolness of her air-conditioned hotel.

Bill's contact met her in the foyer.

'Can you spare me a minute, before you go up?' he wanted to know. 'There has been a hitch with the delivery of the other exhibits. They may take a bit longer than—— Oh, hang on a minute. It looks as if my phone call has come through.'

He followed a signalling waiter, gesturing to Dee to wait where she was, and she sank with a sigh on to a low settee. She felt grubby, tired, and sticky all over, and she longed for the comfort of a soapy shower and a change of clothes.

Her practical cotton top-and-trousers set clung to her damply, and she wondered if it was the done thing in India to invite a male business acquaintance to her room, where she would not be obliged to endure the ordeal of comparing her own dishevelled appearance unfavourably with the pristine condition of other guests waiting round the foyer, who, if they had been out sight-seeing too, showed no signs of its occupational ravages in their sophisticated dress.

The man coming towards her looked as if he had stepped straight out of the proverbial bandbox. Dee threw him a disgruntled look. In contrast to her own crumpled cotton, his cream linen suit bore knife-edge creases down the lengths of his trouser legs, and absolutely nowhere else.

It fitted his tall frame like a glove, hugging broad shoulders and slim hips with the ease of expensive tailoring, and made a perfect foil for the mane of red-gold hair which betokened a fiery nature beneath the cool tone that enquired of her, 'Is this anybody's seat?'

Dee shook her head dumbly. Why did he have to come and sit on the same settee as herself? she wondered irritably. There were plenty of unoccupied seats in the foyer.

She wished her colleague would hurry up and finish his telephone call, and come back and release her to her room. She wished she had chosen to sit in the solitary splendour of an armchair rather than a multi-seated settee. The latter was a large three-cornered affair, and she threw the stranger an inhospitable glance as he lowered himself on to that part of it which brought him into opposite eye contact with Dee whenever she looked up.

His eyes were hazel, she noticed, with odd little glints in them like tiny pieces of quartz. The glints suddenly fired, and she realised she was staring. Confusedly she dragged her eyes away, pretending to be distracted by the sound of a portable radio announcing the latest cricket scores.

'*Cricket!*' she ground out, remembering.

'Don't you follow the game?' the stranger enquired politely, and Dee looked across at him, startled. She had not realised that she had spoken out loud. When she did not immediately reply he repeated patiently, 'Don't you follow the scores?'

'*No!*' She remembered belatedly that she was in India, the home of cricketers *par excellence*, and padded out her sharp monosyllable with a grudging, 'I've got nothing against the game. Not usually, anyway.' His raised eyebrows asked a question, and she answered it with an irate, 'At the moment I'd like to consign cricket to the dustbin!'

His finely cut lips curved upwards at the corners, and he protested mildly, 'That seems a rather drastic disposal of an inoffensive ball game.'

'It isn't the game that offends me. It's the people.'

'The players this season are first class.'

'I don't mean the players. I've got nothing against them. Only the spectators. Or, at least, one spectator in particular.'

The exasperation she had kept bottled up inside her all day, simmering in the intense heat, had had to boil over some time, and it did so now with a rush, triggered by his amused, 'Has your boyfriend stood you up in favour of watching the match?'

Dee glowered. The arrogance of the man, to assume that she, personally, had come second-best to a ball game. She denied stiffly, 'I'm not here with a boyfriend. This man is a business contact I'm supposed to be meeting.'

She wondered fleetingly why she should bother to explain herself to this stranger, but the pent-up frustration found some relief in explanation, and she went on, careful not to go into any detail that would reveal what her errand here was, 'I'm having to kick my heels here, waiting for him to join me. And what happens? He decides he can't come until Thursday because, of all things, he wants to watch a cricket match on Wednesday. The arrogance of it,' she fumed, 'to expect the world to grind to a halt while he indulges his liking for cricket. It's unbelievable. *He* must be unbelievable.'

'You could have a look round Delhi while you're waiting. It's a fascinating city. There is a lot to see.'

'I've tramped all over Delhi today.'

His cool look assessed her dishevelled appearance. 'You look as if Delhi has tramped all over you.'

Dee repressed a gasp of outrage. Whoever he was, the stranger did not believe in being economical with the truth. Before she could think up a suitably cutting answer, however, he turned away from her to signal to a passing waiter, and ordered, 'Iced lime-juice for two, please,' without waiting to see if she was willing to accept his non-offer, or even whether she liked lime-juice or not.

Whoever he was, he did not lack confidence in himself. Dee stiffened her sagging muscles, and retorted with massive dignity, 'I'm not used to this brand of heat.'

'You shouldn't try to do too much until you've become acclimatised. There are easier ways of seeing Delhi than by exhausting yourself. And you need a head-covering.'

He was criticising her now. The cheek of the man!

'I bought a scarf in the bazaar.' Dee could have kicked herself for sounding defensive. She didn't have to excuse herself to anybody, least of all this stranger. 'A monkey stole it,' she finished flatly.

'You've been to see the fort.'

It was a statement, not a question, and for a wild moment Dee had the feeling that the strange flecked eyes had the power to look into her mind. With an effort she pulled herself together. It was evident that the stranger knew Delhi. His 'There are easier ways of seeing Delhi' meant that he had probably used those ways himself, and so it stood to reason that he would be aware of the monkeys.

She managed an indifferent, 'I can buy another.'

Out of the corner of her eye she caught sight of her erstwhile companion hurrying back towards her, his telephone call finished, and she said thankfully, 'Here comes a colleague of mine now,' in a tone that discouraged any further questions from the stranger.

If he asked her what was the nature of her business in India she could not tell him. Parrying such a question might arouse his curiosity, and

if she answered it it could put herself, and the
precious artefacts in her charge, in considerable
danger, and her colleague was returning at just
the right time to rescue her from the dilemma.

Nowadays thieves did not necessarily come
complete with the time-honoured uniform of eye
mask and swag bag. The modern international
variety were impeccably dressed, and highly
plausible. Their ploy was usually to strike up a
conversation with someone they suspected of
being a courier, offer them a drink, and...

Dee threw the cream suit a look of dark suspicion, and, in spite of her raging thirst, she left
the iced lime-juice where the waiter had placed
it, untouched, on the table.

'I'm sorry to keep you waiting for such an age,'
her colleague apologised, sitting down beside her
on the settee. 'The call took longer than I thought
it would. It's not good news, I'm afraid. I shan't
get the rest of the consignment for another ten
days at least.'

Frantically Dee's look signalled to him not to
mention what the consignment consisted of. Did
he not know that he must be discreet? Perhaps
it was the first time he had ever dealt with such
a matter. Perhaps nobody had thought to warn
him. She said quickly, in a desperate attempt to
head off any detailed explanation, 'Then the
cricket match on Wednesday won't matter, after
all.'

'Not now. Indeed, you might like to go to see it together.' Her colleague smiled across at the cream-suited stranger. 'I see you've already met Mr Ransom.'

CHAPTER TWO

THERE was nothing to say. If there had been, Dee felt incapable of saying it. A rising tide of indignation choked her, that Luke Ransom had led her on, allowing her to roundly condemn, in no uncertain terms, all arrogant cricketing enthusiasts, and one in particular—namely, himself.

How he must have laughed as he'd watched her dig a large hole for herself and then fall headlong into it.

Luke Ransom was far from the geriatric antiques dealer she had imagined him to be. He was young—in his early thirties, she judged. He was above-average good-looking—and knew it, she decided sourly. He was also a man of guile, who would need to be watched.

Having lit the fuse, her colleague adroitly dodged the coming explosion. Into the void of silence he announced brightly, 'I'll leave you two to introduce yourselves. Coming!' he digressed as the waiter signalled again for him to take another telephone call, and added over his shoulder, 'I'll be in touch the moment I hear anything definite.'

Before Dee could find words with which to detain him he was gone, and she was left alone with Luke Ransom. She threw him a wary look, while her mind searched frantically for something cool and poised to say, and he denied her the opportunity by enquiring briskly, 'Where is the male courier who is accompanying you?'

'There isn't a male courier. No one is accompanying me.'

'I was told there was a D. Tredinnick.'

'*I* am Dee Tredinnick. D-e-e,' Dee spelled it out clearly with some satisfaction. Clearly this man did not think a mere girl was capable of working as a courier.

He sat upright in his seat abruptly. 'You don't mean—you *can't* mean—that a girl has been sent out here alone on such a mission?' His surprise and anger were as obvious as they were insulting, and Dee's indignation rose to meet his.

'If Bill Williams trusts me, so can you.'

Her tone reduced him to the ranks, but she didn't care. It wasn't any of his business who Bill sent on his missions. This man was nothing to do with WW. He was merely coming along for the ride, at the behest of their Delhi contact. He had no responsibility, and even less authority, so far as she was concerned. With an effort she strove to make herself speak calmly.

'I do assure you, Mr Ransom——'

He swept away her words as if she hadn't spoken. 'Nothing about this business reassures me. Is Bill Williams aware that while you're waiting you'll be turned loose on Delhi, alone?'

The man was impossible! He was everything she had thought him to be, and more. Except old. Dee shot back through gritted teeth, 'Delhi is in no danger from me. I don't bite.'

If anything more were needed, after Alan, to reinforce her views about men, Luke Ransom provided it, she decided angrily.

'I have no fears for Delhi. It is quite capable of looking after itself.'

Implying that she was not. Dee sucked in a difficult breath. 'Mr Ransom——'

'Use my first name. It saves time.'

With royal assurance he assumed that she must know what his first name was. Too late Dee admitted to the knowledge by retorting, 'Luke, then,' and ground her teeth with frustration when the glow in his eyes registered his victory, but he didn't wait for her to continue beyond it.

'I'll call for you at seven o'clock for dinner,' he told her abruptly. Again told, not asked, she registered indignantly as he swept on, 'In the meantime I'll decide on something suitable to keep you occupied while you're waiting.'

With that he flowed to his feet with a lithe grace which made light of the impossibly low settee, and before Dee was able to collect enough of her scattered wits together to enable her to retort he strode away from her, out of the foyer.

He would decide... I'm quite capable of deciding for myself, Dee fumed. In vain she berated herself for not being more assertive, for not making it crystal-clear to Luke that she had neither the need nor the desire for his services until she was obliged to put up with his unwanted company on the flight home.

As for dinner, she had already lost her appetite. She had been looking forward to a peaceful meal, alone and relaxed in her room. Instead it looked like being a confrontation over the cuisine, she thought without humour, and determined that when she met Luke again she would be ready for him, and more than capable of holding her own against him.

To say the least, her unwanted escort was abrasive company, and, drained by the heat and the exertions of her day alike, she did not feel equal to meeting any kind of a challenge this evening.

A blissfully cool shower put her in a calmer frame of mind, and she put through a telephone call to Bill to report on her progress, or lack of it, so far. The time difference caught him just finishing his frugal sandwich lunch.

'Did you say Ransom? *Luke Ransom?*' His cheese and pickle roll failed to muffle his startled ejaculation.

'The same,' Dee confirmed shortly, and outlined the details of their meeting. 'I'm stuck with the man for dinner this evening. But if he imagines he can dispose of my time at the lift of his little finger he's got another think coming. If I have my way we shan't meet up again until it's time to come back to London. That could be another ten days, Bill.'

Dee brightened as a sudden idea struck her. 'Can I come back home, and fly out here again when everything is ready?' she asked her boss hopefully. 'It wouldn't cost any more in the long run. This hotel must be charging a fortune, so it will cancel out the extra air fare.'

'Never mind what the hotel bill comes to. You stay right where you are, and cultivate Luke Ransom for all you're worth,' came back Bill's uncompromising instruction.

'Do I *have* to?' Dee's voice became a wail. 'The man's an arrogant, domineering——'

'I wouldn't know about that. All I know is, in our business, Luke Ransom spells prestige.'

'So does WW.' Dee flew to its defence.

'A double dose never did anyone any harm, so stick with him.'

'What about the exhibition?' Dee shot her last, despairing arrow. 'At this rate, it looks like being over before I get back.'

'I still haven't fixed the venue yet.'

'No joy from Windsor Castle?'

'I'm working on it,' Bill neatly fended her sarcasm, and added firmly, 'Be a good girl, and go along with whatever Ransom suggests.'

'With reservations,' Dee retorted swiftly, and was rewarded by Bill's chuckle from the other end of the line.

'I didn't mean that far, and you know it. But remember, in our line of country being noticed by Luke Ransom is as good as being awarded a royal warrant.'

'In that case, you won't need Windsor Castle for the exhibition, will you?' Dee shot back, and felt better for Bill's laughing 'Touché!' as she put down the receiver.

Her every instinct urged her to remain in her room and avoid having dinner with Luke, but Bill's instruction was clear and could not be lightly put aside, and, reminding herself that the coming ordeal was all in the call of duty, Dee dressed with extra care, using the necessarily limited contents of her suitcase as an armour with which to bolster her confidence for the evening that lay ahead.

It was too hot for jewellery, she decided. She abandoned it, and chose a starkly plain pale green silk sheath dress, drawn softly into her slender waist by a wide white plaited silk belt, and complemented it with matching white linen strap sandals and handbag.

The result looked cool and chic as she descended the wide staircase to meet Luke at the appointed seven o'clock, and, she hoped, hid the flutter of nerves which she despised herself for allowing to tighten her stomach in a manner that made her wonder if trying to eat wouldn't be a waste of time.

Luke watched her descend.

Dee espied him immediately, standing at the far end of the foyer. It would be difficult to miss him. His distinctively coloured hair and his impressive height marked him out from the other men grouped about the foyer, and Dee wished irritably that he would look away from her. His steady regard was unnerving.

So much so that it made her feet feel clumsy, and instinctively her hand went out to touch the balustrade to steady herself. Immediately the tawny head tilted, registering her movement. Guessing its cause, Dee thought vexedly and withdrew her hand quickly to her side, knowing that it was already too late.

Luke moved then. He strolled across the foyer to meet her, and Dee noticed that people automatically parted to allow him free passage.

They both reached the bottom of the staircase at the same time, and for long moments Luke stood there, looking down at her. Dee baulked, unable to take another step until Luke chose to move, and she flashed a frustrated look up into his face in time to see the quartz flecks glowing like bright fireflies in his eyes.

They made the nerves of her stomach tighten still further, with the uncertainty of not knowing for sure what had fuelled the fire. It could have been derision at the brief, revealing evidence of her nerves. It could have been appreciation of her appearance. Luke's voice betrayed neither as he cupped her elbow in his hand and said crisply, 'Shall we go?'

'Do I have any choice?' In spite of Bill's injunction, Dee's voice was barbed, and Luke shot her an oblique look.

'Cease-fire for this evening,' he commanded. 'Some friends of mine have invited us both out to dinner at their home. They thought you might enjoy it better than remaining in the hotel.'

His old school friend, perhaps? Not as old as she had imagined, Dee corrected herself silently, and agreed out loud, 'That was very kind of them,' hoping that her reply conveyed only her gratitude, and not the tremendous sense of relief which flooded over her at his words.

In this respect, at least, she had no difficulty in obeying Bill's instruction to go along with what Luke suggested. Having other company at dinner would help to dilute the disconcerting effect he was having upon her without any seeming effort on his part.

Her skin tingled under the touch of his fingers, and she hoped her unease did not show itself on the surface as she walked beside Luke to the door, steeling herself to resist the sheer male magnetism of the man, which flowed from him in an almost visible aura.

Luke Ransom was no callow university student, nor a small-town sophisticate like Alan. He was a man of the world in every sense, at the very summit of his chosen profession. Rich, powerful, and confident in that power, which drew lesser mortals to him like moths attracted to a flame.

She still found the independently minded Bill's eagerness to make contact with Luke difficult to digest.

She wouldn't be among those whose wings got burned, Dee assured herself, with a flash of self-derision at her own taut nerves as she sat, outwardly composed, beside Luke in the car moments later.

He drove in silence, his attention concentrated on the still crowded streets, through which he twisted and turned with a surety that told Dee he must know every inch of them by heart.

The pungent smoke of a thousand cooking fires made the air hazy, as Delhi prepared its evening meal, and added to Dee's sense of unreality, which became stronger still when Luke finally turned the car into the drive of a large private house, cloistered from the road in a secluded garden.

Luke's friends were evidently people of some substance. He intercepted Dee's glance, and remarked, 'You'll like Manoj and his wife. They both love entertaining, and they're the easiest people in the world to get on with.'

The same did not apply to her companion, Dee thought ruefully, and let out an inaudible sigh of relief that, while Luke had latched on to her nervousness, he had mistaken its cause to be his unknown friends, and not himself.

Her stretched nerves relaxed, and then tightened again almost immediately when he opened the passenger door and, leaning down, reached inside to encircle her arm with lean fingers, to help her to alight.

In any other circumstances, she would have appreciated the courtesy. But, although Luke's touch was light, his fingers seemed to burn into her flesh like red-hot steel, making her wonder for a wild moment if their imprint might leave matching blisters to mark where they lay.

With an effort she forced herself to concentrate on what he was saying as he went on conversationally, 'They both work in the hospital near here. Manoj is an expert on tropical diseases. He's coming over to the UK on a lecture tour to the main teaching hospitals, later this month. Gita is a gynaecologist. They've got two little boys, but I expect they'll both be in bed by now, so we shan't see them tonight.'

His tone expressed regret, and Dee sent him a look from under her lashes. So the domineering tycoon had a weakness. He was evidently fond of children, or at least the two belonging to his friends.

Had he got any children himself? she wondered. She had heard somewhere that Luke Ransom was unmarried. She had supposed him to be a crusty old bachelor. How mistaken could she be? But being a bachelor did not necessarily mean...

Hastily Dee switched her thoughts into safer channels. Luke seemed to have an uncanny ability to latch on to what she was thinking, and she had no desire to boost his ego by showing the slightest interest in his private life.

She was her own woman and she intended to stay that way, and she had no objection to him reading that thought if he wanted to.

He gave no sign of having done so when he added, 'Never mind. You'll see the boys tomorrow. They're a delightful pair, and great fun to be with.'

Dee stiffened. Tomorrow?

Luke was taking a lot for granted. Like the fact that she would fall meekly in line with any plans he made to fill her time until the exhibits were ready to collect. In spite of Bill's instruction, she did not intend to offer herself as a doormat for Luke to tread on.

His intuition had let him down badly on that score, she decided, and opened her mouth to make it clear that she had her own plans for the disposal of her free time, and those plans did not include Luke.

She got so far as a firm, 'Tomorrow I'm going to...' when the door of the house opened, and their host and hostess appeared to greet them, cutting off her own personal declaration of independence at source.

'How good of you to come!'

Manoj and Gita ran down the steps to greet them, and Dee liked them both on sight. The tall, slender expert on tropical diseases, with his grave, intelligent face and eyes that smiled a warm welcome as he shook Dee's hand, and his wife, shorter, plumper, with a merry glance, and two outstretched hands that caught at Dee's eagerly as she exclaimed, 'I'm so glad to have you! Now I shall be saved from another evening of having to listen to endless talk about cricket.'

'Cricket?' Dee could not help it. She burst out laughing, and Gita giggled, her merry look telling Dee that her hostess knew all about her recent gaffe on meeting Luke, but somehow she did not mind Gita knowing, and their shared amusement formed an immediate bond between them.

The laughter helped Dee to relax and forget her nerves, and dinner became a lively meal. Manoj and Gita were both widely travelled, as was Luke, and Dee listened, fascinated, as the talk ranged from one end of the world to the other, the others speaking with easy familiarity of all those places which she had promised herself she too would one day go to see.

She was not allowed to remain merely as a listener, however.

'Tell us about your work,' Gita urged, and, encouraged by her obvious interest, Dee joined in the conversation with accounts of her journeys on Bill's behalf.

In the company of his friends Luke became a different person. Gone was the austere, domineering tycoon of her brief acquaintance, and in his place emerged a carefree man who enjoyed playing with his friends' children.

He teased her and Gita with gentle impartiality, and took up the conversational cudgels against Manoj in a good-humoured argument which they both enjoyed, and Dee watched covertly as the tiny quartz flecks flared, and died, and flared again as the talk ranged from the serious to the hilarious and back again.

She experienced a distinct sense of shock when the meal came to an end, and she realised that almost three hours had passed since they had first arrived, and later, while they sat finishing their coffee in the couple's charming drawing-room, her host claimed virtuously, 'Luke and I haven't mentioned cricket once, all the evening.'

Gita chuckled. 'You've both showing withdrawal symptoms.' She turned to Dee. 'Manoj and the boys are all mad about cricket, so you can see that I'm badly out-numbered. When Luke joins in as well I simply don't stand a chance. Oh, go on,' she laughed at the two men who, incredibly, managed to look like guilty schoolboys, 'go on, switch on the radio. You know you're longing to hear the latest scores. Come on, Dee. Let's make ourselves scarce. We'll go upstairs and look in on the boys, and talk about something interesting, like clothes.'

'Your sari is beautiful,' Dee ventured as her hostess led the way, and Gita confessed,

'I've got the best of both worlds. I wear Western dress quite often, for convenience. I love the Paris fashions,' she twinkled, 'although, of course, I can't afford them too often.'

Gita would look stunning in whatever the *haute couture* houses of the world could offer, Dee thought silently, and said out loud, 'The embroidery is exquisite.'

Gita smiled. 'After I've been working at the hospital all day, and wearing a plain white coat the same as the men, I like to change into something pretty in the evening. I like to stop being a doctor, and become——' she paused to choose her words '—and become just a woman.'

'Not *just* a woman,' Dee protested, vehement in spite of herself, and Gita cast her a swift look.

'Are you a feminist?'

'No.' Dee's denial was equally forceful. 'I haven't got any time for that sort of thing. It always seems, well, sort of strident somehow. And unnecessary.'

'Completely unnecessary.' Gita nodded agreement. 'However much people try to change things, women will always be women, and men will always be men, and...'

'*Vive la difference!*'

'Exactly,' Gita laughed, and placed her finger to her lips as they paused opposite a door. 'I'll go in and check on the boys. Come with me if you'd like to see them. I don't want to bore you with children...'

Her look asked a question, and Dee answered it simply, 'I'm never bored by children.'

Her smile carried conviction as she looked down on the sleeping pair, and Gita pointed to each of the small beds in turn.

'Four years old, and not quite six. They don't look anything like so angelic when they are awake.'

'They're both lovely.' Dee's eyes softened as she looked down on the two small sleeping faces, and heard herself say, with a feeling of surprise, 'You are so lucky.'

'Perhaps you will have children of your own soon.'

'Oh, no. Not for a long time, anyway.' Dee regained control of her errant tongue, and insisted, 'I don't intend to get married. I want to travel and see the world.'

The reason was her secret, and not to be shared.

Gita said quickly, 'Manoj and the boys are my world.'

Dee sent the other woman a curious look. Gita had travelled much more extensively than she had herself. Was she really content with domesticity after that? She had her career at the hospital as well, of course. Dee stirred restlessly, and offered, 'My brother's wife is expecting her first baby at any minute. By the time I get back home

I shall probably have acquired a niece or a nephew. I can't wait to know which.'

'It isn't the same as having a baby of your own. Are you betrothed?' Gita's eyes slid to the ring finger on Dee's left hand.

'No.' She shook her head emphatically. 'I don't intend to sacrifice my freedom.'

How nearly she had done so, to a man who was unworthy. Dee thrust aside the memory, and Gita consoled, 'You will meet someone one day. And then it won't seem like a sacrifice.'

Dee's, 'Mmm,' was non-committal. From now on she had other things to do with her life that did not include men. The reason brought the tension back to claim her as she followed Gita downstairs and rejoined the men in the drawing-room in time to hear Manoj mourn, 'There won't be any more score announcements until tomorrow.'

Dee countered Gita's unrepentant 'Hurrah!' with a smiling, 'Is your team playing?'and her host surprised her with,

'I don't follow a team.'

Gita explained, 'Manoj and Luke are both purists. They don't give their allegiance to any particular team. Only to the game.'

It took a particular brand of self-assurance to be so impartial, and Dee sensed that this was an attribute which both men shared.

'Never mind,' Gita consoled them. 'You've still got Wednesday to look forward to.' She turned to Dee. 'Manoj and I decided to take a break before the lecture tour starts. We've handed over to our deputies at the hospital, and the boys have been given leave by their school, so they will be free to go to the match as well. They won't escape lessons altogether, of course. They'll be having a tutor for so many hours each day.'

'I'm sure the outing on Wednesday will soften the blow,' Dee smiled, and thought gleefully, That disposes of Luke on Wednesday.

It would still leave tomorrow and Tuesday, for which he appeared to have already made plans that included herself, and for which, high-handedly, he had not seemed to think it necessary to seek her approval first.

He's got a shock coming, Dee promised herself, but found she was unable to think of a plausible excuse when Manoj cajoled, 'Will you allow us to show you something of Delhi tomorrow, Dee? Luke tells me you will be free, and he says you haven't seen much of the city so far.'

'Oh, I couldn't possibly encroach on your holiday,' Dee protested, and her host smiled.

'You would be doing us a favour. Gita in particular.' He sent his wife an affectionate look. 'She is something of an historian, and nothing pleases her more than to show off our famous monuments to a visitor.'

He went on proudly, 'Gita is an excellent guide,' and added as a further incentive, 'The boys will be coming with us, too. If they can help it they never miss one of their mother's walk-abouts, as they call them. They are already showing signs of Gita's sense of history. They can't wait to come to England. Luke has promised to take some time off to be their guide.'

How could she refuse?

Without saying a word himself, Luke had driven her into a corner from which there was no escape. Dee threw him a frustrated look, and their glances met across the room, and locked. The quartz flecks flared triumphantly, confirming that it was Luke who had engineered the invitation. Dee felt the sour taste of defeat in her mouth, and found her usually alert mind equally devoid of ideas for an excuse when Gita added her plea to that of her husband.

'Do come with us, Dee. We'd love to have you. We'll take you to see the Taj Mahal. You'll love that. And the fort.'

'She's already been to the fort, and had her headscarf stolen by the monkeys,' Luke put in, and amid the general laughter which followed Gita offered generously,

'I'll lend you one of mine.'

Luke brought the scarf with him when he called at Dee's hotel to collect her the next morning.

'Thank you.' She took the tissue-wrapped package and slid it open, and gave a gasp of pure pleasure as she unfolded the long length of embroidered silk.

It looked new, as if it had never been worn. Perhaps it was one of Gita's best scarves? By a happy coincidence it matched the basic colours of Dee's cotton trousers and top, freshly laundered overnight to their original crispness.

'It's lovely. How kind of Gita.'

Dee draped its gauzy beauty across her dark hair, and flicked the one tasselled end over her shoulder in the approved manner, and Luke agreed, 'Very lovely,' with a long look which brought a ready flush to her cheeks, and made her wonder if he meant the scarf or...

She was given no time in which to pursue the thought, because Luke went on immediately, 'You won't need a head-covering quite so much today. We'll be using a minibus. It's air-conditioned, so you should find your sightseeing a lot more comfortable.'

And, true to Luke's intention, she would not be doing that sight-seeing on her own. 'Turned loose on Delhi' was the way in which he had phrased it. His choice of words still rankled.

His steady regard was making her feel the reverse of comfortable, and it was a relief when Manoj and Gita and the children came to join them.

The two men took it in turns to do the driving, and at first the children were quiet, evidently under constraint from their parents to be on their best behaviour, Dee diagnosed, but her friendly overtures soon restored the boys' normal exuberance, and they chattered gaily as Gita led the small party round her favourite monuments.

Dee thanked her warmly for the loan of the scarf.

'It isn't one of mine,' Gita denied. 'Although, of course, you would have been more than welcome to borrow one. But Luke wanted to get you one himself. He thought you might like it to keep, as a souvenir of your stay in Delhi.'

'He didn't tell me that it was from him.'

It explained why the colours so exactly matched those of her cotton trouser suit. She should have suspected, knowing that Luke was bound to have a noticing eye for detail such as colour, but she'd had no reason to imagine that he might give her a gift. The fact that he was giving her his time he probably regarded as a patronage.

He had allowed her to accept the scarf, thinking that it was on loan from Gita, knowing that once she had worn it she would not be able to return it, and would be obliged to keep it, not as a reminder of her stay in Delhi, but as a reminder of him.

Why?

On past experience she was unlikely to have any further contact with Luke after they returned to England. Perhaps, like all powerful people, he enjoyed wielding that power over others, even in minor things like the wearing of a scarf.

She had good reason to know that Luke was an adroit manipulator when he wanted to get his own way, and within the constraints of Bill's instruction Dee determined to evade that way, whatever it might be, as much as possible.

The two posed a conflict that kept her nerves on edge in spite of the temporary armistice between them, and the light touch of the scarf across her head and shoulders felt uncomfortably like the dominant touch of Luke's hand upon her, which the intense heat would not allow her to shrug off.

In spite of the comparative coolness of the minibus, they were obliged to leave its shelter at intervals in order to explore, and then it was much too hot for her to abandon the scarf and go bareheaded, and it remained, a gossamer reminder of Luke's victory, that brought with it a moment of pure panic at the ease with which he had taken control.

CHAPTER THREE

THE morning of sightseeing presented Dee with a Pandora's box of sights and sounds, which she enjoyed in spite of Luke, and which were to remain forever in her memory.

Delhi sparkled. Gita brought its history to life, and the children bombarded their mother with all the questions which Dee might have hesitated to ask for herself.

'Gita's in charge today. I'm just the chauffeur.' Manoj good-humouredly conceded the stage to his wife, obviously proud of her expertise, and just as obviously enjoying what he must have heard many times before.

'It's fascinating. None of the guidebooks give as much detail as this,' Dee answered, enthralled.

It was a day of contrasts. Cool marble and shady stone made a blessed relief from the fierce heat and dust of the streets. The insistent call to prayer from a nearby mosque cut across the raucous din of the markets, and the tinkle of temple bells dropped a melodious chime into their ears, as soothing as the sound of a falling fountain.

'Don't you envy the bride?' Gita teased her as they paused to watch a wedding procession go by.

The cars were gay with garlands of lilies and marigolds, the colours as cheerful as the crowd, who laughed and waved to the happy couple and their guests.

Dee laughed and waved too, but her head-shake was vehement. 'Envy her? Certainly not. I told you, I intend to stay solo.'

She was aware of Luke watching her, listening to the small exchange, but she didn't care. Her plans for her life were nothing to do with him, and she didn't allow his quizzical look to spoil her enjoyment when he stationed himself by her side, the better to point out detail she might otherwise have missed in the crowded thoroughfares.

The challenge of Luke's presence heightened Dee's sensitivity, and honed her powers of observation to an acuteness which nearly matched his own, and it soon became a silent contest between them, all the fiercer because it remained unspoken, as to who should be the first to notice things.

Dee pointed gleefully. 'Look! There's a snake charmer. Over there, by the foot of the market steps. He's got a rattlesnake,' she guessed wildly, squinting against the glare towards the living rope that swayed to the piped music, horrifyingly close to its owner's face.

'That rattlesnake is a cobra,' Luke scored another point triumphantly, and Dee bit her lip in vexation.

It was a cobra, of course. Her tongue seemed fated to put her in the wrong with Luke. But then, he knew Delhi, and she did not, she excused her defeat.

By tacit consent they both abandoned their verbal sparring when they drove to see the Taj Mahal, their own conflict dwarfed by its tragic history.

Dee gazed in silence at the glittering marble structure. Its reflection was blurred in the stretch of wind-rippled water which made a long mirror below it. Like the tears that must have blurred the sight of the grieving husband who had had the monument built in memory of his wife. Dee felt a lump rise unbidden in her throat as Gita recounted the story, and she felt no shame at her own emotion.

She could contemplate Romeo and Juliet, and all the other great lovers of history, with a detachment that left her unstirred. The Taj Mahal was different. Here was genuine heartache, locked in stone, the pain and the desolation of lost love frozen into its glistening walls. A monument to human anguish, mocked by the unfeeling sunshine.

The tenderness and the tragedy caught at Dee's heart-strings, still raw from memories of her own recent unhappiness, and when Gita remarked quietly, 'Now there is a *real* love story,' she blurted out with a bitterness she could not quite control,

'To be loved like *that* would be almost worth giving up your freedom for.'

'Almost? Not quite?' Luke enquired sardonically from beside her.

Dee flashed him a defensive upwards glance, and then looked away again quickly, unable to meet the glowing quartz flecks that, even when she averted her face, continued to burn down on to the top of her head, penetrating the flimsy protection of the bright silk scarf, and leaving the unanswered question dangling like a tossed gauntlet between them.

A threatening storm ended their sightseeing abruptly shortly after lunch. The heat began to build up to suffocating proportions, and Dee visibly wilted.

'It's time you had a rest,' Luke decided masterfully, ignoring her protestations and adding, 'I'll expect you all to dinner this evening. I'll collect Dee from her hotel.'

He smiled down at the two hopeful-looking children. 'It will be long past your bedtime, I'm afraid. But I'll make up for it. I'll buy you both an ice-cream on Wednesday.'

Luke was domineering, but he could be kind when he wanted to be, Dee reflected later as her weary body obeyed Luke's commands, even though her rebellious mind willed otherwise, and she drifted off to sleep in the grateful coolness of her air-conditioned room at the hotel while she tried in vain to push away the suspicion that it was as much Luke's presence as Gita's expert guidance which had made Delhi sparkle for her that morning.

Dinner was a memorable meal, as much for the surroundings in which they ate as for the food itself. In deference to his two Indian guests, Luke chose vegetarian for himself, although to Dee's surprise he made no attempt to influence her own choice.

Nevertheless she tuned into his reason and intuitively followed suit, and silently derided herself for her quick flash of pleasure as she met Luke's glance of approval from across the table.

In an attempt to divert her thoughts she fixed her concentration on her surroundings. Bread and water would become nectar and ambrosia in a place such as this, she thought, awed by the splendour of the magnificent room.

Luke had brought them to his own hotel for the meal. 'It was a palace once,' Manoj enlightened Dee, and she thought tartly, Where else would the king of the antiques world stay but a palace? And then felt ashamed of her sarcasm when Manoj added wistfully, 'So many of our palaces have had to be turned into hotels in order to earn their upkeep. Just like your own ancestral homes in the UK. It's sad, in a way, although it does preserve their splendour for future generations to see.'

'This is magnificent. Out of this world!' Dee exclaimed, making no attempt to hide her admiration, and, obviously pleased, Gita offered,

'I can tell you its history if you like. That is, if you haven't heard enough of history for one day?'

'Do tell,' Dee urged.

History was safely in the past, done with and unalterable, the perfect antidote to the turmoil and uncertainty of her own thoughts, which she pushed thankfully into the background while Gita obliged, and ancient tales of love and war and derring-do occupied most of the rest of the meal, until at the end Dee confessed, 'I wish Bill could bring his exhibition over to India and hold it here. It's so much more romantic than at home.'

Luke's look derided her choice of words, and she flushed hotly, wishing them unsaid, but Luke made no comment, merely questioning, 'Isn't he using the National Exhibition Centre? He usually does.'

Dee raised mental eyebrows. For someone who so consistently ignored the services of WW, Luke seemed to be remarkably well informed about the firm's activities. She answered off-handedly, 'Not this time. He's looking for an exotic background to match the exhibits. I suggested Windsor Castle,' she dimpled.

Gita chuckled, but Luke took her up with a quick, 'Has he got any particular venue in mind? Apart from Windsor Castle, I mean?'

'He hadn't when I spoke to him on the telephone last night.'

'That must mean the date for the exhibition hasn't been finalised yet, either.'

'Only in broad terms. It will be some time towards the end of the month. Nothing specific as yet, so far as I know, because when relies upon where.'

'Mmm.'

Luke looked thoughtful, and Dee sent him a searching look. Was the 'Mmm' dismissive? Uninterested? Critical? How dared he criticise her firm, whose services he consistently rejected?

Manoj broke the slight silence which had fallen by applauding, 'That is good. It means the exhibition will still be running while we are in the UK. I would like to take Gita to see it.'

'It would be cooler over there than if you held it here.'

Gita's smile teased Dee, and she admitted ruefully, 'I thought I could cope with heat. But Delhi at this time of the year produces a brand of its own.'

'You would get used to it, in time.'

'I shan't be here for long enough.'

'The monsoon heat makes us wilt, too,' Manoj consoled, and Gita said,

'We're going to stay in the hills for a few days, for a short break before Manoj starts his lecture tour. Why don't you come with us? There's plenty of room in the bungalow, and we'd love to have you. We shall be starting off as soon as the men get back from the cricket match on Wednesday.'

'I'd love to come,' Dee answered promptly, 'but there's just the chance that the exhibits might arrive on time after all. I must be in Delhi for when they come.'

'Luke said they would be another ten days. That means at least a fortnight in India,' Gita returned with accepting frankness, and Luke cut in with a decisive,

'You'll have plenty of time for a trip into the hills. Leave your telephone number with your contact here, just in case, although it won't be necessary. Gita's right on target about the timing.'

So was Luke. His arrows scored the target of her pride, and made her want to shout at him, 'No, I won't leave my phone number. I won't be told where to go and what to do by you, as if I were an employee.'

She didn't doubt that the offer of a holiday in the hills had been engineered by Luke, as had the sightseeing tour this morning. He was determined to dispose of her waiting time in the manner in which he thought fit, and his success so far rubbed her pride raw.

But—another fortnight of enduring the heat of the city and she would surely melt. The only

alternative, if she was to insist upon remaining
in Delhi, would be to stay in the air-conditioned
hotel, which left her with the choice of dying of
boredom, or dying of heat.

The hills offered temptingly cool air, and a
blessed escape from the destructive, breathless,
end-of-monsoon humidity.

The choice was no choice at all, and, avoiding
Luke's eyes, Dee capitulated, 'In that case, I'll
come. The heat *is* getting at me, but it seems such
a waste to spend the waiting time hiding away
from it in the hotel,' making it seem as if it were
her own decision, and not Luke's, that she should
go. The heat was making her feel limp, but surely
in the modern air-conditioning of the restaurant
it shouldn't have accounted for the sudden feeling
of depression that latched on to Luke's choice of
words?

'*You* will have plenty of time.' Not '*we* will
have...' Did it mean that Luke wouldn't be
joining his friends for their holiday in the hills?
Dee should have felt relieved, but instead a flat
feeling of anticlimax kept her silent as Luke drove
her back to her hotel at the end of the evening.

His, 'See you on Wednesday, Manoj. I'll be in
Calcutta until then,' confirmed that Dee would
be on her own for the next couple of days.

Having demonstrated his power to dispose of
her as he thought fit, cynically Luke had no
compunction about leaving her stranded when it
suited him, Dee condemned him unjustly,

chagrined to discover that the prospect of freedom, in which she would have rejoiced a few hours earlier, now gave her a completely irrational sense of desertion.

She didn't see Luke again until Wednesday afternoon, when he and Manoj and the boys returned from the cricket match, but in the meantime his kiss remained with her, burning her lips, hotter than the Indian sun, and from which there was no protection when he left the imprint of himself upon her mouth, like a brand to reinforce his taunting, 'I'll be back...'

His gesture when he stopped the car outside her hotel caught Dee wholly by surprise, and, taken unawares, she had no defence against him. He silenced the engine, and, turning swiftly in his seat, he caught her in his arms in one fluid movement for which, her thoughts turned inwards, she was totally unprepared.

'Goodnight, Dee,' he murmured.

His head was a descending silhouette above her, his lips a demanding firmness on her mouth that cut off her stammered thanks for the dinner, took away her breath, and exploded a million stars in her dazed mind, which far outshone the brilliance of the night sky above them.

His kiss laid siege to all that she had been, all that she intended to be, and all the plans she had made for her own unfettered future. Under its onslaught Dee felt her defences begin to waver.

Student kisses she had coped with, too numerous to count. Even with Alan she had always been able to remain in control. Under Luke's kiss she felt her control begin to slip away. Desperately she fought him, but her lips pursed under his with a life of their own, which defied her efforts to check them, and fear sliced through her like a knife.

As he felt her response Luke's kiss changed and deepened, exploring the soft contours of her mouth, and the laughter dimple at the one corner, which was not laughing now. Dee thought wildly, This isn't what Bill meant when he told me to go along with Luke.

Bitterly she remembered her own confident, 'With reservations.' Luke had none, and was laying siege to her own, and her small, beating fists were no defence against him.

The thought of Bill steadied her. It acted as a lifebelt to her drowning senses, and frantically she clung to it, and used anger as an anchor.

How dared Luke assume that he could use her lips as if they were his to command, just as he had taken control of her time? How dared he assume that both belonged to him, simply because he had agreed to be her escort on a purely business mission?

He had had the effrontery to criticise Bill for allowing her to remain in Delhi while she waited for the rest of the artefacts to arrive, but Luke himself posed more of a threat than any city she had yet encountered.

She strained backwards, away from him, but his hold upon her was too strong for her to break free, and her struggles were ineffectual against him.

'What's the matter? Doesn't the free and independent career girl like being kissed?' he taunted.

His mockery proved the last straw. It drew a strangled sound from Dee's dry throat. She *did* like it. Or at least her errant lips did, although she would die rather than allow them to admit it. Instead she forced them into forming one word that shot, bullet-like, through set teeth.

'*No!*'

'Not by me? Or not by anybody? You said you hadn't got a boyfriend.'

Why had she told him that? Why had Luke remembered? What was left of Dee's scattered senses told her that he would remember everything, and use it to his own advantage. If only she had invented a fiancé to provide her with a watertight excuse, but if she tried to dredge one up at this stage it would leak like a colander, and Luke would know that she was afraid.

Of him? Or of herself? She pushed away the conundrum, and stammered, 'Not by anybody. *Let me go!*'

The arrival of the hotel commissionaire saved her. Footsteps approached the car door on Dee's side, a hand reached out to open it for her, and she left her seat with a speed that caused her to stumble and nearly fall when her feet hit the ground.

Luke's mocking, 'I'll be back,' rang in her ears, which registered the sound of the car engine starting up again as she fled up the hotel steps without looking back.

She hadn't meant to, but she turned at the top, unable to help herself, and bit her lips in vexation at the sight of Luke's raised hand, which told her he had seen her through his rear-view mirror and knew she was watching as he steered the vehicle expertly out into the flow of traffic on the busy main road and was quickly swallowed from her sight.

Dee was trembling all over when she reached her room. Angry with herself, and furious with Luke, she kicked off her sandals, flung her scarf and handbag on to the bed, and sluiced her face at the wash-basin, but no application of soap and water, or rubbing with the thick, soft towel, could take away the throbbing from her lips, which ached with the merciless pressure of Luke's kiss, and ached the more because it had been so soon removed.

Dee prowled the room, too restless to read, too highly strung to think of sleep. She knew she ought to ring Bill and report on her progress. She even reached out for the telephone and lifted the receiver, but then replaced it, her bemused mind unable to cope with telephone calls tonight.

She must pull herself together before she spoke to Bill. He knew her too well not to sense when something was amiss, and if he started to question her she might not be able to successfully cover up the reason why she was *distraite*. Her nerves felt raw from her encounter with Luke, and she couldn't endure to be teased about it.

As if it could read her thoughts, the telephone bell shrilled loudly.

'*Oh!*' Dee started violently. For a shocked moment she stared at the noisy instrument, her eyes dilating. Was it Luke ringing her? Nonsense! How could it be? Unless, that was, he had an in-car telephone. Even so, there was no reason why he should telephone her when he had only just left her.

Was it only just? It seemed like an age ago. A glance at her watch told her that it was less than ten minutes.

Perhaps it was Gita? Maybe something had cropped up at the hospital, which meant that they would have to postpone their break in the hills, and they were ringing to let her know. The mundane reasoning steadied Dee, and gave her the courage to lift the receiver.

'Dee Tredinnick . . .'

'Dee, at last! I've been trying to contact you for the past hour.'

'Bill? What are you ringing me for?'

It was always the other way round. The couriers rang back to base from wherever they happened to be, to report progress to their boss. It was only in an emergency that Bill ever rang them himself.

'Is anything the matter?' Dee wanted to know. 'You don't sound like yourself somehow. Has the exhibition been cancelled?'

She tried to iron out the sudden hope in her voice. If the exhibition was cancelled she could go home without encountering Luke again. The prospect didn't bring with it the expected feeling of relief, and Dee closed her eyes, unable to cope with the turmoil of her own conflicting thoughts, which hoped the exhibition had been cancelled, and at the same time prayed that it had not. Through a thickening fog she heard Bill say, 'I don't feel like me. No, the exhibition hasn't been cancelled. It's very much on. In fact, everything in the garden is lovely, and you are absolutely my favourite flower.'

Dee's eyebrows climbed. Her normally unflappable boss sounded positively excited.

'Have you been drinking?' she asked him suspiciously.

Bill never did drink. The only liquid Dee had ever known him to consume was coffee. One heaped teaspoonful of instant, and two ditto of sugar, stirred into the disgraceful old crock mug with the faded Mickey Mouse pattern on it that no amount of money in the bank could part him from.

'What's up, Bill?' Dee demanded ungrammatically, and his chuckle came clearly across the line.

'Nothing's up yet. But it will be, from next month. I'm going to double your salary.'

'Now I know you've been drinking.'

'Hand on heart, I haven't touched a drop. But I intend to celebrate with a glass of bubbly with my cheese bun as soon as I'm off the telephone. This is really something to celebrate.'

'If you don't stop burbling nonsense, Bill Williams, I'll put the phone down. What is going on, for goodness' sake? What is it you're supposed to be celebrating?'

'Don't tell me you don't know?'

'I'll give you just ten seconds to make sense, or else... One, two——'

'You really don't know, do you? Ransom hasn't told you?'

'Told me *what*? Bill, I warned you. Three, four——'

'That fella knows how to keep his own counsel, that's for sure. He rang me less than an hour ago, and offered me his own home, would you believe? It's one of the old ancestral type, too—he actually offered me his own home, to stage the exhibition in. Just like that. Out of the blue.'

'He...did...*what*?'

Dee's voice rose in a squeak, and Bill confirmed, 'It's a fact. How on earth did you manage to persuade him, Dee? Ransom Court beats Windsor Castle any day, at least for our purposes. It's right bang in the middle of the Chiltern Hills. And it couldn't come at a better time of the year, with all those beech woods turning colour. It will be just great,' he enthused. 'The ideal setting. It's near enough to London to be easy for people to reach, and far enough out to be right in the country.'

Dee scarcely heard him. The tremble extended to her knees, and she sat down suddenly on her bed. So that was what Luke's 'Mmm' had meant. And he hadn't breathed a word of his intentions to her, not even when he was bringing her back to the hotel in his car.

Did he think he was being clever, or what? Or did he regard her, a mere courier, and a woman into the bargain, as being of so little importance that it was unnecessary to mention his plan to her? Bill's voice reached her through a fog of mounting anger.

'I haven't actually accepted Ransom's offer yet.'

'Why not? Don't you want to? You said——'

'You bet I want to. It would be a real feather in WW's cap. No one has ever managed to breach Ransom's defences before, to my knowledge. Not even the Press.'

'Then what's stopping you?'

'You are.'

The gravity in her boss's voice riveted Dee's attention, and she frowned.

'Why me? What have I got to do with it?'

'Before I accept Ransom's offer I want to know what lies behind it. I don't know quite how to put this, Dee...'

'Try it straight,' she told him tersely, and felt her anger mount as Bill went on soberly,

'When I told you to go along with whatever Ransom suggested I didn't mean it literally. You know I don't expect you to—er—overstep the mark in the course of duty.'

'So that's it.'

A hysterical desire to laugh fought with an urgent desire to smash something. What had Luke said to Bill to make her boss wonder...? The hysteria won, and Dee exploded, 'Bill, you goose! No, I haven't overstepped the mark, as you so delicately put it. Nothing would induce me.'

'Ransom's a handsome devil.'

'Devil' was an excellent description, Dee thought sourly, but said out loud, forcefully enough to convince her listener, 'You ought to know me better. It will take a lot more than good looks to part me from my freedom. I'm being polite to the man in the course of duty, and that is all. You've got absolutely nothing to worry about in that direction. Far from being seduced, I don't even like Luke Ransom.'

'Thank goodness for that!' Bill's gusty sigh of relief blew through the line. 'It means I can accept his offer with a clear conscience. They say the whims of the mighty are unpredictable. Maybe he just fancied showing off his home, for once.'

'The whims of the mighty have usually got strings attached to them,' Dee retorted ungraciously.

'There don't seem to be any attached to this one. Unless you can call the fact that he wants you along to help organise the exhibition a string.'

'He wants *me*?'

'You're beginning to sound as if the needle's stuck.'

'But the couriers never have anything to do with the actual exhibitions.'

'There's always a first time. And this one is not to be missed. I'll have a special sweater designed for you, with WW emblazoned on the front, so that people can see we've reached the top of the tree.'

If Luke expects me to sit and sing in the branches, and to his tune, he's got another think coming, Dee promised herself grimly as Bill rang off, and wondered impatiently, Who on earth can it be now? when the telephone shrilled again.

It was Gita this time. She said, 'Dee, I should have mentioned this earlier. You'll need a warm sweater when we go into the hills. Don't forget to bring one along with you. It can get chilly up there, morning and evening.'

'I won't forget,' Dee promised in a muffled voice that gave vent to laughter, which seemed, oddly, to verge on tears when she put the receiver down, and told herself shakily, At least this sweater won't have WW emblazoned on the front.

That was still to come. No matter what Bill might believe, there had to be a price for Luke's offer, and the coin was to be her own freedom for the duration of the exhibition. Dee felt as if a trap was closing round her.

Once again Luke had taken control, and man-oeuvred her slyly into a corner from which she could not extricate herself without the risk of damage to Bill and his firm, and Dee bitterly re-sented this further demonstration of his deter-mination to exert his power over her.

She felt again the hard circle of his arms sur-rounding her, their steel strength laughing at her ineffectual struggles to be free, and irritably she tried to shrug the feeling away, but it persisted, a disturbing echo of the pain which beset her lips and refused to go away.

The day that followed was far from the haven of peace which Dee had anticipated. The heat seemed to be more exhausting, the sun more glaring now that she had no distraction but her own company, and the places she visited lacked the extra dimension of interest posed by the chal-lenge of Luke's company.

No matter how she drove her feet to walk round the obligatory tourist sights, she could not outdistance her mind. It refused to function on the same receptive level which it had achieved while Luke was there to challenge her powers of observation, and became instead a confused battleground of anticipation and dread at the prospect of meeting him again.

The ensuing war left Dee feeling mentally battered, and she had still reached no conclusion by the time Wednesday arrived.

Luke came to see them off after lunch. The children danced round Dee, excitedly vying with each other to tell her about the morning's outing, until their mother commanded them sternly, 'Spare her, do. Not everyone is as mad about cricket as you are.'

'Uncle Luke gave us our ice-cream,' they digressed obediently, and Dee nodded.

'He didn't forget.'

She had experience of Luke's memory herself, and stiffened defensively when he strolled up to join them after helping Manoj to stack the luggage in the minibus, then contrarily felt deflated when he gave her no more than a casual, 'Hello,' and turned immediately to beam his attention on the excited children.

'You two are next,' he told them, mock ferociously, and gained squeals of delight when he swung them high in his arms and pretended to toss them after the suitcases into the back of the vehicle.

His kiss was gentle enough, however, when they raised small faces to his, before he handed them over to their motherly ayah, who was to accompany them on the holiday.

Watching him, Dee wondered at the strange mixture that could allow a man to be so gentle one moment, and so ruthless in wielding his power the next. She wondered if he would mention his telephone call to Bill, and decided stubbornly that, if Luke didn't raise the matter, neither would she.

It was Luke's place to tell her, not the other way round, and if he didn't consider her important enough to be taken into his confidence on a matter which concerned them both she wouldn't give him the satisfaction of showing curiosity.

In spite of her determination, however, she couldn't help feeling piqued when the moment of departure came and Luke still remained uncommunicative. As soon as the children were safely settled in the van he turned to kiss Gita and the ayah, and shook hands with Manoj, and Dee turned away to climb into the bus and take her place beside the boys, when the pair chorused, 'You haven't said goodbye to Dee, Uncle Luke. You mustn't miss Dee out.'

Dee went rigid. Was Luke's omission deliberate? Would he have missed her out if the children hadn't noticed? Desperately she wanted him to, and just as desperately she did not, but what she wanted seemed to be of little consequence to Luke.

'We mustn't miss Dee out,' he agreed gravely, and the repetition was both a challenge and a mockery, underlined by the bright quartz glow in his eyes that stared down into her own with the heat of a living fire.

Dee moved convulsively, jerking away from him, her eyes wide with the anticipation and the dread which had haunted her for the last two days, but she was not nearly swift enough to evade his outstretched hand.

With it he turned her to face him, and his strength set her stiff resistance at nought. He lifted her bodily towards him, holding her aloft as easily as if she were no heavier than one of the children, while he unhurriedly planted a kiss, four-square, on her trembling mouth.

As the minibus pulled away Gita said regretfully, 'It seems such a pity that Luke isn't coming with us.'

'Perhaps he'll be able to join us when he finishes his business in Calcutta,' Manoj hoped.

Dee remained silent. Her host and hostess did not have the benefit of Luke's taunting whisper, 'I'll be back,' which had been designed to reach her ears alone, and had acted like a probe to set her every nerve-end tingling when he'd finally released her into the minibus, and she bemusedly obeyed the children's clamour to, 'Wave goodbye to Uncle Luke, Dee.'

Obligingly Dee raised her hand, knowing that it was not really goodbye, but only a brief *au revoir*.

CHAPTER FOUR

LUKE would come. But when? The question haunted Dee, in the days that followed, like the wraith of the man himself.

To keep it at bay she threw herself into frantic activity with the two boys, and they welcomed her into their games with enthusiasm. The ayah was willing enough, but her plump roundness, that made such a comforting lap for the two children when they were tired, made her less than fleet of foot.

Dee was able to chase with them after their speeding ball, run alongside them as they flew their brightly coloured kites, and still have sufficient energy left for hectic games of tag.

But no matter how hard she played, or how fast she ran, Dee discovered that she could not escape Luke's whispered promise, 'I'll be back.'

Promise? Or threat?

It came between her and the games she played with the children, bringing down their derisive laughter on her head when she dropped their balls and absent-mindedly missed her turn at board games.

'You're miles away,' they accused her. 'Tell us where you'd gone to.'

'To never-never land.' With an effort she made a fun thing of it, grateful that the boys were still too young to be able to detect the forced note in her laughter.

Luke's image dogged her footsteps like a reflection of her own shadow when she accompanied the boys and their ayah on their daily walk to feed apples to the ponies that grazed in a nearby meadow, and it sat with her like a mischievous sprite at bed time, taunting her with the unanswerable question, When? Will he come tomorrow? Or the day after?

In the cool hill air Dee's flagging energy revived, and the fact that her spirits declined to follow suit made her increasingly impatient with herself. It was madness to allow Luke—any man—to dominate her thoughts in this manner. It threatened her self-sufficiency, as well as her peace of mind.

She had imagined herself to be strong enough to keep that mind uncluttered, and fixed with a singleness of purpose upon her goal, to keep herself free from male entanglements and dedicate her life to travel. But Luke was proving to be stronger than she had bargained for, and it was humiliating to find his personality imposing itself upon her thoughts, even when he himself was absent.

'It doesn't look as if Luke's going to make it after all,' Manoj regretted on the third day of their holiday, but still Dee's eyes continued to watch for his arrival, no matter how hard she tried to control them, and as the hours passed she became tense and irritable, and increasingly nervous that her host and hostess might notice her distraction and imagine that she was not enjoying herself.

Luke arrived shortly after breakfast on their fifth day in the hill village.

A helicopter appeared, and hovered low over the open space of a small golf course, which had been built to cater for the growing tourist population. The children spotted the machine from the bungalow veranda.

'It's Uncle Luke! It's Uncle Luke!' they shouted, and raced to watch the machine land, hotly pursued by their ayah, calling anxious instructions to them not to get too close. Fighting a feeling of inevitability, Dee followed more slowly, with Gita and Manoj.

She responded mechanically to Gita's pleased, 'This is nice. Now we can all be together again for a few days, before we go on the lecture tour.'

Luke had come, just as he'd said he would. Just as she had known he would. Even before he stepped down from the machine, Dee knew that it had come to bring Luke, and no one else.

A door opened in the side of the aircraft, and her heart gave an uncomfortable lurch as his familiar tall outline darkened the space.

Take three deep breaths, she told herself, reverting to her father's advice for coping with stress. It had always worked before, quickly restoring her ability to face whatever the situation demanded.

It did not work with Luke.

The lurch turned to a swift, uneven beat, which accelerated as he jumped agilely to the ground and ducked under the still whirring rotor blades. He scooped up the two boys, one under each arm, and ran with them away from the dust cloud raised by the machine.

As soon as he was clear the helicopter rose again into the air, and Luke held up the boys to wave to the pilot as it clattered away to lose itself over the nearest hillside, then he returned the children to their feet and strolled towards their parents and Dee, announcing unnecessarily. 'I'm back.'

He spoke to Gita and Manoj, but his eyes as he said it turned on Dee. Her breath came faster, in time with her accelerating heartbeat, and she tried to look away, but found she could not as the glowing quartz flecks mesmerised her, and she thought bemusedly, Maybe tonight the imp will let me sleep. And knew that she hoped in vain since, while Luke's return had answered one question for her, it threatened to pose at least a dozen more, not one of which she wanted to answer.

However reluctant Dee was to admit it, in the days that followed Luke's presence brought the sparkle back, just as it had in Delhi.

The challenge of his company brought her to life in a manner that left her both dismayed and exhilarated. No matter how her mind urged caution, she could not help but notice that the carpets of wild flowers in the surrounding meadows took on a brighter hue when Luke walked with them to take tit-bits to the ponies each morning.

The already spectacular scenery seemed to become even more majestic when he named the distant peaks to add to her enjoyment of the view, and the clear, crisp air took on a wine-like quality, which doubled her restored energy.

It showed itself in the easy dexterity with which she caught balls tossed by the boys, which she had dropped before, and would surely have done so again had Luke not shouted to her commandingly, 'Catch it, Dee! Hold it!'

Her fingers could do nothing less. Obeying his call, they reached up and plucked the flighting ball from the air with an ease that astonished her, even as they closed round the bright sphere.

'You're getting better,' the boys encouraged. 'You haven't dropped a catch at all today.'

'I was only rusty. I haven't played ball games since I was at school.'

Those games had never held the thrill of these, whose sole rule seemed to be to keep the ball in the air, and if it was dropped, or someone else caught your throw, you lost a point.

'Get rid of it quick, Dee. Throw it!' the children shouted, and Dee drew back her arm and made a less than expert throw in Luke's direction.

The two groaned in unison as he raised his arm for the easy catch, and then cheered wildly when, inexplicably, he dropped it.

'Another point to you,' they gloated, and Dee forced a smile and ran with the children to retrieve the ball, with vexation pursuing her because she knew that Luke could have held on to the ball easily enough if he had wanted to, and it was condescending of him to allow it to drop in order to let her score a point.

The kind of condescension which a grown-up would extend to a young child, although Luke hadn't done so with either of the boys, tacitly acknowledging their masculine supremacy in the matter of balls.

Dee hugged the vexation to her. It made a good armour. It made her better able to cope with Luke. Sternly she reminded herself that, if she was to travel the world as she intended, there were bound to be many more such encounters with men of the world like Luke, who would be just as handsome, just as virile, and just as dominant as he was.

To remain free, and to know any peace in that freedom, she must learn to handle their undoubted charisma, and to remain untouched by it, and by them. To do this successfully, she realised belatedly, she must first learn to handle herself.

When deciding on her future, after Alan, she had naïvely left out the most important ingredient from her calculations, that of her own essential femininity, which had responded to the first really powerful male challenge in a way that both surprised and frightened her.

No one, not even Alan, had ever succeeded in arousing her like this. It was the difference between meandering along a country road and driving in the fast lane of the motorway, and she would need to keep all her wits about her, and her eyes firmly fixed upon her way ahead, if she was to survive to reach her destination.

Luke would make excellent practice, she told herself robustly, and wondered with an inward grin what he would think if he knew he was unwittingly taking on an apprentice.

The small amusement restored her poise, and gave her enough confidence to take Luke to task when they finally abandoned the game in favour of lunch.

'There was no need for you to be so patronising. I'm quite capable of scoring my own points without your help.'

'I don't doubt it.' His level regard made Dee feel, uneasily, that she was being strident. It made her wish she had not spoken, but it was too late now, and Luke heightened her discomfort with a cool, 'It wasn't my doing. The boys wanted me to let you gain a few points so that you wouldn't feel left out of it. They meant to be kind. They're too young, yet, to appreciate feminine independence when they see it,' he mocked.

His manner derided her independence, and her. Dee felt her cheeks begin to burn, and grow hotter because Luke's sideways glance registered their colour and told him that his shot had gone home. It went deeper than he realised, Dee thought ruefully. It probed the question, Would Luke have been equally kind if he hadn't been pressed to be by the children? Or would he have grabbed the chance to take advantage of her own lack of expertise and triumph over her, as she knew that he could have done with ease?

Dee didn't know, and she couldn't ask, and suspected from the enigmatic look which Luke turned on her face that he had guessed her question, and had no intention of providing her with the answer.

He had still not mentioned his telephone call to Bill. Dee comforted herself with the reflection that, in that respect at least, she was one step ahead.

She already knew what Luke obviously still regarded as a closely kept secret, and if and when he finally condescended to share it with her she promised herself that she would respond with an uninterested 'Yes, I already know', and immediately turn the subject, and leave Luke feeling as deflated as she herself did now.

The subject came up unexpectedly the next day.

Dee sat with her host and hostess, finishing a leisurely after-lunch coffee on the bungalow veranda. The two children had been taken by their ayah to play with some young friends at another bungalow, and Luke had left his coffee on the low table between his chair and Dee's while he'd gone to answer a telephone call. He returned shortly afterwards, and unhurriedly finished his cooling drink before informing Dee, 'That was your Delhi contact ringing me.'

'Ringing *you*?' Not herself, as he should have done.

'Yes, he's got all the exhibits together now, so I told him to arrange our flight for tomorrow.'

'*You* told him...'

Dee choked on her own coffee, but Luke went on as if he hadn't noticed, 'If we check out of our hotels first we can pick up the package and go straight to the airport from the bank. It will cut down the risk if we don't have to carry the exhibits through the city twice.'

Her pride was more at risk than the package, Dee thought furiously. Her Delhi contact had telephoned Luke, and not herself, as if it were the natural thing to do. Her fingers closed convulsively round her coffee-cup in a white-knuckled grip, but before she could speak Gita exclaimed, 'I'm so looking forward to seeing the exhibition! I do hope it won't be held too far

away for us to be able to reach it in between
Manoj's lectures.'

'I've decided to hold it at Ransom Court,'
Luke told her. 'You'll be staying with me while
you're in the UK, so you'll be able to view the
exhibition at your leisure.'

He had decided, not Bill had decided. As if
Luke had the sole right to decide on anything he
wanted for everybody, and expected no oppo-
sition to whatever decision he chose to make.
Mounting rage made an iron band tighten round
Dee's chest.

Luke did not even bother to look at her as he
gave her the news. He dropped it as a *fait
accompli* right into her lap, and left her to digest
it as best she might, with no opportunity to say
'I already know' and turn the subject, as she had
planned.

Dee's churning mind registered, He's said
nothing about wanting me to be there for the
duration of the exhibition. Had he forgotten? Or
was this just another example of his arrogant assumption that her agreement was not necessary?

In a tight silence she listened to the conversation going on round her. Manoj offered generously, 'You can borrow the minibus to drive
you back to Delhi if you like, Luke. You could
send it back by chauffeur.'

'Thanks, but there's no need to deprive you of
it. While I was about it I arranged for the 'copter
to come and fly us back. It will be quicker than

going by road.' He turned to Dee. 'If you haven't flown by helicopter before it's no more alarming than flying by plane.'

Dee did not care if they travelled on elephant back. The thing that alarmed and infuriated her was the lordly way in which Luke had taken control of the arrangements, which should have been left in her hands alone, as the courier in charge of the mission. At the very least, he should have had the decency to consult her first. Instead he acted as if she were his subordinate, there to do as she was told.

The mere fact that her Delhi contact had phoned Luke and not herself fuelled her indignation to boiling-point, and she held the lid on the simmering cauldron with difficulty while Gita mourned, 'What a pity you've had to cut short your holiday here with us. Manoj and I had planned on us all having another few days together.'

A pity? Dee's teeth clenched until her jaw ached as much as her tightened fingers. The pity was that she had consented to come in the first place, and put herself in a position where she had no option but to spend hours in Luke's company, albeit along with the two children and their parents.

Beguiled by the place and the people alike, she had foolishly allowed herself to relax and be lulled into a false sense of security, confident that she could handle Luke's company, like fine wine, and suffer no ill-effects from the draught.

Too late she realised its potency.

Too late she wished she had been more assertive, more independent, more aloof, and because she hadn't Luke had grabbed the advantage and taken over her professional responsibilities as well as her personal time.

With angry self-condemnation Dee took a gulp of her coffee, which rewarded her hasty mouthful by going down the wrong way.

'Ouch!' In the midst of her splutters for air Luke's hand came down hard in the middle of her back, sending the errant liquid along its proper route with painful speed.

'Did you have to make that quite so hard?' she muttered furiously as soon as she recovered her breath.

'Sorry.' The tilt of his lips said he wasn't in the least sorry, and Dee's return glare held all the bottled-up anger and resentment she felt against him.

He narrowed his eyes, reading the anger and the resentment, and knowing their cause was not only the smack, but Dee didn't care. These days even Bill didn't trouble to give her detailed instructions. He merely outlined her assignment, and left her to take charge of the rest herself, and Luke had absolutely no right to usurp her freedom to do so.

She opened her mouth to tell him so, when Manoj remarked, 'You must make your last day here memorable. Do something special. Is there anything you'd particularly like to do this afternoon, Dee?'

There were several things she would like to do, all of them unmentionable because they included Luke's swift dispatch to some other, preferably far distant, corner of the globe, but before Dee could think of a more acceptable reply the object of her wrath answered for her, 'Dee is coming riding with me.'

She thought wildly, He can't dictate to me like this. I won't let him. I'll tell him I don't ride. That I hate horses. Anything, but I *won't* go riding with him.

She hadn't been alone with Luke since the night he had taken her back to her hotel in his car. And then he had kissed her. The memory of it stung her lips still, and the prospect of being alone with him again appalled her.

Her new-found confidence wavered. How would she cope if Luke tried to kiss her again? How would she cope with herself? Horses were of no use as chaperons.

Dee fought for calm. If her refusal was to be effective it had to be dignified, and final. She began determinedly, 'I'm not——'

Luke cut across with, 'While the children are out Manoj and Gita will be able to have the whole of the afternoon to themselves. They may not get another chance to be alone again until after the lecture tour is over.'

Dee could have groaned out loud. It had been a fatal mistake to wait, even for a few seconds. Like a hawk swooping on its prey, Luke had snatched the advantage and denied her the right to make her own choice.

With careful deliberation Dee drew in three long, painful breaths. She felt as if her mind was spinning out of control. With one deft stroke Luke had made it impossible for her to refuse to go with him. Equally impossible for her to remain with her host and hostess and intrude a third person upon their precious privacy.

He used every single opportunity, with infuriating success, to bend her, Dee, to his will, and foil any attempt to protest on her part as neatly and effectively as he had scored points in the ball game. Only this was not a game. This was for real, and the consequences spelled disaster to Dee's dream of independence.

Into a stretched silence Gita said, 'I didn't know you rode, Dee,' and with an effort Dee forced her voice into a reluctant admission.

'I ride a good deal when I'm at home.'

'How did you know I could ride?' she demanded of Luke when, less than an hour later, they mounted two beautifully groomed polo ponies, borrowed from the nearby club.

'It wasn't too difficult.'

Was anything difficult, let alone impossible, for this impossible man? Dee urged her mount up beside Luke's across the short hill turf, refusing to allow her escort to lead the way and to meekly follow behind him, as he no doubt expected her to do. He slanted her a sideways look.

'When we've been with the children to feed the ponies, you've handled the animals as if you'd been doing it all your life. And they responded to you, as they would not have done to anyone who wasn't used to horses.'

Dee's lips tightened. She would need to guard her every movement while she was with Luke. Nothing escaped his notice, and he used every scrap of knowledge to his own advantage.

The drumming of hoofs coming from somewhere just ahead of them lifted her head enquiringly, and Luke identified the sound for her with, 'The polo ground is quite close. The track we're following skirts round the edge of it. Let's go and watch them play for a while.'

'If you want to.'

Dee tried to keep the eagerness out of her voice. She was not interested in polo. But a match meant people, and she welcomed any relief from the nerve-stretching ordeal of being alone with Luke.

Typically her mount sensed the tension in its rider, and reacted with a skittishness which demanded Dee's full concentration to hold it on course and prevent it from bumping into Luke's impeccably behaved pony on her other side. The animal's nervous fidgeting served to increase Dee's irritability, and when Luke remarked, 'I've been approached about setting up a polo ground at Ransom Court,' she grasped at neutral ground to ask,

'Do you play?'

'Now and then. I don't have a lot of time. I'm away from home a good deal.'

'Like now, I suppose?' Dee said, and blurted out before she could stop herself. 'You didn't tell me you'd offered to hold the exhibition at Ransom Court.'

A second later she could have bitten her tongue for allowing Luke to see that his secrecy bothered her, but it was too late now to draw back, so she cast caution to the winds and demanded, 'What made you do it?'

Luke cast her a long, considering look, assessing her tone as much as the words she had spoken. His eyes seemed to bore down into her head, probing her mind, but stubbornly Dee refused to look up to meet them.

She was conscious of her own heightened colour, painfully conscious of Luke's nearness, which turned into actual contact as her pony took advantage of her temporary distraction to sidle close to its fellow.

In the process it pressed her leg against Luke's. Instantly Dee checked the move with a quick pressure of her knees, but not before the sensuous feel of hard muscle pressing against the length of her calf sent tingles shooting through it, which dyed her cheeks to an even deeper hue, the brighter for the quick flash that lit the quartz-flecked eyes as they interpreted her desperate look.

After what seemed a year of time Luke drawled, 'Bill Williams didn't leave me any option.'

'*Bill* didn't?' Dee flashed a look of pure astonishment. 'Bill told me you'd telephoned him to make the offer. Out of the blue, he said.'

'Not quite out of the blue.' The drawl was pronounced. 'I reckoned if Bill Williams was as careless of the safety of the exhibits as he is of the safety of his couriers then my choice of venue for the exhibition had got to be better than his, from a security angle. Some of the pieces in the Indian exhibit belong to people known to me professionally, and I decided it was time I took a hand in the arrangements myself.'

The thought flashed across Dee's mind, He's concerned for the exhibits, and his business relationships. Not for me. Out loud, she exploded indignantly, 'Bill is *never* careless, either of his couriers or of the valuables in their charge. We all have the most thorough training in security.'

'From where I'm sitting...' Luke's eyes slid over Dee's slight figure with insulting calculation. 'From where I'm sitting, to send a five-foot-nothing female to escort a priceless collection of gems is worse than careless. It's criminal folly.'

'*Female*'! Not 'girl'. Not 'woman', or 'lady'. But '*female*'. And she was an inch or two taller than five feet. Dee ground her teeth with fury.

'I am quite capable of——'

'Being hijacked, mugged, or worse,' Luke finished for her.

Dee knew a swift relief that he did not detail what the 'worse' might entail. The relief died in mounting anger, and she flashed, 'Male couriers face exactly the same risks as the women.' Not the 'worse', but certainly the other two. And she refused to repeat the 'female'.

Her retaliation produced no noticeable retreat on Luke's part. He commented blandly, 'A man is better able to take care of himself than a girl.'

Of all the male chauvinistic...

Before Dee could sort out her thoughts into suitably cutting words Luke added, 'Bill Williams seemed a bit reluctant at first, I thought. But I told him if he'd got another venue booked to cancel it. He agreed, of course.'

'Oh, of course,' Dee agreed sarcastically.

She sent a fixed stare between her pony's ears. She knew the reason for her boss's hesitation, if Luke didn't: Bill had the kind of integrity and care for his staff, in spite of what Luke might think, that would not accept this most marvellous solution to his problem until he knew that he could do so with a clear conscience.

She swung in her saddle to justify Bill's hesitation, and the movement blinded her to the one on the ground. The snake struck viciously at the pony's hoofs, a split-second before Luke roared, *'Dee, look out! Look out...'*

He was just that split-second too late. The evil head flashed out of a patch of rough scrub growing at the side of the track, and Dee's pony gave a shrill whinny of fright.

Luke's hand shot out, grabbing for the animal's bridle. His fingers brushed leather and closed on air as the pony jerked its head away with a stiff-legged jump that would have done justice to a jack-in-the-box.

Seeing its quarry in retreat, the snake struck a second time, and, giving a shrill scream of fright, Dee's mount bolted at top speed straight towards a shelter belt of trees which shaded the polo ground on their other side.

Dee's rider instinct took over. The animal's ears were laid back flat against its head, its eyes glazed with terror, and it had the bit firmly fixed between its teeth.

Dee didn't waste time trying to pull it in. The pony was a lot stronger than her own arms, and low-slung branches rushed to meet her, waiting to crash into her and sweep her out of the saddle. She leaned low across her mount's neck, and kicked her feet free from the stirrups.

The loose leathers flapped wildly, bouncing the irons up and down and serving to increase the animal's panic, but it couldn't be helped. It was better than the risk of being dragged, if she should become unseated.

The wind rushed in her ears. The hammer of hoofs beat a tattoo of impending disaster upon her senses. The tattoo increased in volume. Perhaps the polo game was starting up again? And then Luke was beside her, the louder tattoo coming from the hoofs of his own pony.

He rode with the agility of an Indian brave. Strong thighs clamped his tall body to his pony's back, as if he were part of the animal. As he raced up alongside Dee he leaned across, and even *in extremis* her frightened eyes could appreciate the supple arc of his body as he reached out both arms to grip her round the waist.

Her pony tried to veer away, but with superlative skill Luke kneed his own mount round in a tight turn. With any other horse a spill would have been inevitable, but the nimble-footed polo pony, accustomed to such manoeuvres, took the abrupt change of direction in its stride.

It did what Luke intended, and forced Dee's mount round, and then the two animals were racing shoulder to shoulder away from the peril of the trees, back into the open, running neck and neck up the steepest part of the already steep slope in a calculated bid of Luke's to slow the wild, uncontrolled flight of the bolting horse naturally, without any need to pull it in by force.

It was a classic piece of riding skill, executed with the precision of a ballet sequence, and orchestrated by the drumming hoofs. Through a daze Luke's command penetrated Dee's ears.

'*Let go!*'

Her numb fingers obeyed his order automatically, without any reinforcing message from her brain. As the reins dropped she felt herself being lifted high out of her saddle, and shut her eyes as she floated for a moment on nothingness. And then Luke straightened in his saddle, and with one arm he moulded Dee to his own body, while with his other hand he sought for, and regained control of, his own reins.

'That was a fine piece of riding, Ransom.'

Dee opened her eyes. Men surrounded them. Young men, carrying mallets, and mounted on ponies similar to their own. The unseen polo team? Their spokesman confirmed her bemused guess.

'We abandoned our game when we heard you shout, and came to see what was the matter.'

'Weren't needed,' another observed laconically, and enquired, 'Are you all right, miss?'

Dee managed to nod. Her voice refused to function. How could she say, in truth, that she was all right, when Luke's arm continued to press her against him, the clean, chiselled line of his jaw nestled lightly on her tumbled hair, sending electric signals to its very roots?

Her nostrils caught the faint male smell of his exertions as her face pressed against his sweat-dampened shirt, injecting a liquid fire into her veins more potent than any snake bite, and in-

finitely more dangerous, since there was no
known antidote.

Dee's pulses raced. Their wild gymnastics
caused the surrounding sea of faces to advance
and recede in a manner which warned her that,
if Luke was to set her down, her legs would refuse
to hold her.

Violent trembles shook her, and she hoped fervently that her rescuer would put them down to
her recent fright. She didn't want to admit, even
to herself, that her convulsive shivers were triggered as much by the vital attraction of the man
who held her as by the emergency just past.

The polo team crowded round, eyeing her
anxiously, and, embarrassed, Dee made a small
convulsive movement to free herself as pride
came to her rescue and restored her voice.

'I—I'm fine . . . really . . .'

It was quavery, and uncertain, but it seemed
to satisfy the riders.

'That's the spirit,' they applauded. 'You're in
no more danger now.'

No more danger?

Dee longed to shout at them, 'Luke Ransom
is more dangerous than any bolting pony,' and
had to grip her teeth tightly together in order to
prevent the words from spilling out.

Branches might lie in wait to sweep her from
the saddle, but the impact of hard arms threatened to sweep away her senses, and broken bones
were preferable to a broken heart. One experience in that direction was one too many, and

not to be repeated. With a rising sense of panic, which equalled that of her blowing pony, Dee hissed at Luke, *'Loose me!'*

He must have heard her, but he didn't deign to answer. His only response was to tighten his grip round her midriff, and with mounting frustration Dee heard one of the polo players offer, 'Your pony still seems jittery. I'm going back to the stables now. If you like, I'll lead him in for you.'

'I can ride him back.' Dee tried ineffectually to struggle free from Luke's grip.

'It's risky, miss. After bolting like that something might easily spook him again until he's calmed down properly.'

His description could apply as much to herself as to her pony, Dee thought raggedly, and steeled herself to insist, when Luke cut in, 'Thanks. I'd be grateful if you would. We'll ride back slowly, in tandem.'

In tandem.

Dee stiffened in Luke's hold. How typical that he should choose such a phrase. Loosely translated, in tandem meant falling into line and following meekly behind wherever the person in front chose to lead.

Her plans for her future did not include falling meekly into line behind any man, ever again.

CHAPTER FIVE

THE after-glow from the sunset seemed to linger for a long time.

Dee lay back wearily in her chair on the veranda, and watched the glow slowly turn the distant snow-covered peaks from scarlet to orange to a delicate icing-sugar pink. Reaction set in from the afternoon's events, and she felt suddenly drained of energy.

She had listened with a feeling of disbelief when Luke had recounted their adventure to their host and hostess during dinner and unexpectedly given her credit with, 'If Dee hadn't been such a good horsewoman the results could have been very much worse.'

Big of him, she thought sarcastically. The last thing she expected was to receive an accolade from Luke. With an effort she resisted the temptation to bow an acknowledgement across the table, and answered instead, with matching honesty, 'If you hadn't steered my pony away from the trees it would have been disastrous.'

Give the devil his due for services rendered. Like saving her life. Dee harboured no illusions as to what the outcome might have been if a branch had swept her to the ground at such a speed. At the very least, Luke had saved her from severe injury. At the worst... She shivered, and added, 'Luke turned him just in time.'

It was an oblique way of offering her thanks to Luke, which she could not bring herself to make more fulsome. If he hadn't so high-handedly engineered the ride in the first place it wouldn't have happened. Now it had, and owing him her life and limb put her under an enormous obligation, which gravelled her pride.

It also left Luke wide open to expect something from her in return, and so effectively closed the door against her planned attempt to get Bill to send one of the other couriers in her place to help organise the exhibition at Ransom Court.

Manoj observed sympathetically, 'You look absolutely shattered, Dee. And no wonder, after such a dreadful experience. You should have an early night, to recover. You've got a long day ahead of you tomorrow.'

It would seem even longer spent in Luke's company, Dee predicted gloomily, and consoled herself that at least they couldn't be alone together on an aeroplane.

Going to bed early tonight would be the perfect excuse to limit the time still further. She raised her hand to smother a yawn that wasn't entirely fictitious, and confessed, 'I shan't need rocking tonight.'

She had been rocked to the core already by her own unwanted reaction to Luke, and no matter how much she tried to convince herself that the fright and upset had made her extra vulnerable, and so lowered her resistance to him, she knew that, however tired she might be, rest would be hard to come by when she eventually went to bed.

She envied the children their ability to drop into dreamless slumber almost the moment their heads touched their pillows. She had helped Gita to tuck up the two earlier in the evening, and as she'd bent down to kiss them goodnight the four-year-old had told her drowsily, 'We had a lovely afternoon, Dee. I played with the puppy. It went like this.' He gave a squeaky imitation of a puppy's cry, which ended in a wide yawn, and Gita smiled as she shut the door behind them.

'They won't be any trouble for the rest of the night. I'll look in on them later in case they need tucking up again, but I don't expect they'll move after such a hectic day.'

She got up from her chair now, intent upon her motherly task, and Luke rose with her, saying, 'I'll come, too. I brought the boys a jigsaw each from Calcutta. If I put the parcels at the end of their beds they'll find them when they wake up in the morning.'

'You spoil them,' Manoj smiled, and got up too as the telephone shrilled a summons from the hall. 'I'll get it. You two go in to the boys. Will you be all right on your own for a few minutes, Dee?' he asked courteously, and she nodded.

'Of course. You go and answer the phone before it wakes the children.'

Silence dropped round her as the others went about their tasks, and Dee let herself relax. She hoped Luke wouldn't return before Gita and Manoj. She didn't feel equal to coping with any more of his sole company today. If he did come back, she promised herself she would plead tiredness as an excuse to go to her room. She would have Manoj's advice to back her up, and Luke could not argue with that.

Long shadows had stolen the icing-sugar pink from the mountain peaks, but there was still sufficient reflected light left in the sky for Dee to be able to make out vague shapes in the carefully tended garden of the bungalow.

Something stirred in the shrubbery, and alerted her attention. Another snake? She strained her eyes anxiously. As she watched, a thin whine broke the silence, followed by a shuffling sound, and a small, pale shape, on four unsteady legs, blundered among the bushes. It sank down under one of them, near enough for Dee to be able to recognise what had made the sound.

She could have laughed out loud. A dog! It must be the one the children had spoken of, which they had been playing with that afternoon. Evidently it had followed them back from their friends' bungalow, and had got itself lost in the garden. Dee ran down the veranda steps, forgetting her tiredness.

'Here, boy! Come to me.'

She held out her hands towards it coaxingly. It seemed to be having some difficuly in extricating itself from the tough stems of the closely packed shrubs. Perhaps its collar had caught on one of them, and was holding it back? She bent forward to see, just as Luke grabbed her up in his arms and held her clear of the shrubs and of the whining dog.

Unconsciously her mind had registered his footsteps, racing at top speed towards her across the lawn, but, intent upon the animal, she had taken no notice.

And then he was upon her, like a whirlwind, his arms scooping her up and carrying her high off the ground, back towards the bungalow.

'Have you gone mad?' she cried angrily. 'Put me down this minute.'

He ignored her. Without pausing, he whirled round and ran with her towards the bungalow steps. She saw the dog lunge forward and sink back again, and then she had no time to notice anything more as Luke took the steps in one heart-stopping bound, and didn't release her on to her feet until they were safely back on the lamplit veranda.

'Are you crazy?' Her eyes blazed up into his.

He shook her words to a stop. 'Did you touch the dog?'

'I didn't get anywhere near the dog, thanks to your grabbing me up as if I were a sack of potatoes.'

'You make a very pretty sack of potatoes.'

His flippancy was the last straw. 'How dare you haul me in from the garden in that manner? Who do you think you are?'

'Would you believe, your guardian angel?'

Gaoler, more like. Dee pulled in air through clenched teeth, but before she could draw in enough to propel a vehement 'No, I wouldn't' back into his face, Luke hurried on, 'It's high time you were in bed. You heard what Manoj said. We've got an early start tomorrow.'

His arrogance was insufferable. 'What right have you got to tell me to go to bed? I'm quite capable of taking care of myself, without your help. Since when did you turn ayah?'

'I will if you want me to. Just say the word,' Luke invited her softly.

Dee's breath was a sharp hiss that resembled the sound of the snake, but her churning mind was incapable of drawing comparisons.

Luke's teeth were a white flash above her, and coming closer. His parted lips were a mocking invitation, but for some reason, his smile failed to reach his eyes.

Even through her anger, Dee was quick to notice that the quartz flecks remained unlit, leaving his eyes curiously cold and bleak, and there was a taut rigidity in his body as he pressed her to him that was at odds with his jaunty manner.

'Well?' When she didn't answer Luke put two fingers under her chin, and tilted her face up to meet his, refusing to allow her to take refuge in silence, and, cornered, Dee stammered, 'No...I...you...'

What right had he to fling impossible questions at her, and then demand answers which she did not want to give? Anger came to Dee's aid, and she grasped control of her stumbling tongue, and forced it to answer firmly, 'I went to get the dog. It must have followed the children, and now it's lost.'

The dog wasn't the only one that was in danger of getting lost. Trapped in the tight circle of Luke's arms, she was rapidly losing her own direction, and wandering around in a darkness of his making. She needed to get back on course fast, before her reeling senses lost sight of her resolve.

Luke said, and his voice sounded oddly rough, 'Manoj is looking after the dog. Leave it to him. That's what his telephone call was about. You've got better things to do.'

Evidently the dog's owners had missed their pet, and phoned round their neighbours to find it. But taking it back to them would mean that Manoj might be away for some time, and Gita, too, might be a while attending to the children,

Dee realised with an unease that lent an edge to her voice as she snapped, 'Such as?'

As soon as she had spoken she wished the words unsaid. They acted like a burnish to bring life back to the quartz-flecked eyes, which burst into a fire that warmed the tension from Luke's body. His hands moulded her to him, and his voice murmured, 'Such as thanking me for rescuing you this afternoon.'

His lips bored down on to her mouth, exacting the thanks with interest. Frantically Dee tried to twist her head away, to free her lips from the shock waves of sensation which started from the contact and flooded through her whole being.

She felt herself drowning in the flood, helplessly carried away on a tidal wave of feeling that swept away all thoughts of the dog, of Manoj and Gita and the children, and left only herself, and Luke.

He was behaving like a savage...a monster...a *man*, and the dormant woman inside Dee, which Alan had signally failed to arouse, uncurled itself like a sleeping tigress, and rose to meet the onslaught.

How different this was from what she had once believed to be love! The difference swept away her defences, and with a tiny moan her lips parted under the relentless pressure of Luke's kiss. Dee felt herself begin to go pliant in his arms, responding with a passion she didn't know she was capable of as her body arched to meet his, exchanging kiss for kiss.

Dark shadows marked Dee's eyes the next morning, betraying her restless night. Sleep eluded her until late, and when it finally came it brought with it no rest.

'Now, do you want me to help you to bed?' Luke taunted when he finally released her.

Dee put up a hand to cover her quivering lips, pressing back the answer that instinct demanded should be 'Yes. Yes, I do', and reason sternly warned her must be 'No!'

Luke laughed, a triumphant sound, deep in his throat like the growl of a tiger, reading the answer he wanted in her wild eyes, and mocking it. The laugh acted like a knife to cut away the bonds which bound her, and, with an inarticulate cry that was neither yes nor no, Dee wrenched herself free from his hold, fled to her room, and pushed the door hard shut behind her.

Even with the barrier firmly between them, she found she was unable to shut out the image of her tormentor. He was there in her dreams, in which she clung desperately to her bolting pony, fleeing not from the snake, but from Luke, who pursued her relentlessly, always gaining on her, and calling out, 'I'll be back...'

She awoke trembling and damp with perspiration, 'spooked', as the polo player had so succinctly put it, just like her unfortunate pony. Her head ached with tension, and her lips with shame for having been so weak as to betray her by returning Luke's kisses.

Her heart winced at the memory, warning her that it, too, risked suffering the same pain again, only this time much worse, unless she could remain strong to pursue her chosen path, and didn't allow herself to weaken and turn aside, tempted by distractions along the way.

Luke was a distraction, and worse.

As slumber finally came to claim her her drowsing mind registered a sharp, explosive sound, coming from somewhere close by. She listened for a while, but it was not repeated.

Perhaps it was a car backfiring. It was late for travellers, but people were coming and going among the holiday bungalows all the time. Maybe someone had been entertaining and let off a firework? In this fascinating land of many cultures firecrackers seemed to be an inseparable ingredient of any celebration.

The helicopter arrived late the next morning, delayed by a thick mist which shrouded the hillsides, making it impossible for the machine to land.

'Will this mean you'll miss your flight, Luke?' Gita worried, and Dee thought desperately, We mustn't miss the flight. It would be too cruel. The quicker she could get away from the relaxed holiday atmosphere of the bungalow, the better. Relaxed was a misnomer. Her nerves felt as tight as an overwound watch spring, and she longed to plunge back into the safety of her normal, hectic, workaday world.

There she would have no time in which to think about anything but the hundred and one problems which presented themselves unasked, and which would, she hoped, leave no room for Luke in her mind.

She wouldn't be able to force him out of her life until the period of the exhibition was over. Roll on the day! she wished fervently as Luke answered his hostess, 'The sun should soon burn off the mist. Anyway, we're booked on an early-evening flight, so we've got time to spare.'

An early-evening flight meant hours yet to be spent in Luke's sole company. Swiftly Dee reversed her wish, and hoped instead that the mist would hang about until the last possible moment, to allow her to remain in the company of Gita and her family, who until now had acted as an efficient buffer between herself and Luke.

She dreaded the thought of meeting him at breakfast-time, and she had left it until the last possible moment to leave her room and join the others. She didn't know how she would meet him, how she would look, or behave. She felt as if his kisses had left a mark on her lips, clear for all the world to see.

Even more unnerving, how would Luke behave?

Dee's hand trembled as she opened her bedroom door and forced her reluctant feet in the direction of the veranda, but Luke's cool, 'Good morning,' gave no hint of what had passed between them the evening before.

It was a studied rebuff, and anger—as much against herself as against Luke—rose to stiffen Dee's resolve.

That was another lesson she needed to learn, and the quicker she was able to absorb it, the better she would profit by it. Kisses meant nothing to a man beyond the brief satisfaction of the moment.

No doubt Luke had slept like a log last night, dreamless, uncaring, while she had tossed and turned, haunted by a myriad conflicting emotions, not one of which would trouble the man who was the cause of them.

Dee accepted her cup of breakfast coffee, refused food, which she felt would choke her if she tried to swallow it, and made her excuse to Gita, 'It's too early in the day for me to eat.'

She turned aside to help the younger boy slot together the first pieces of his jigsaw. The bottom outline of the picture was sharply defined, as befitted his age group, but he complained. 'I can't see how all these bits are going to fit together to make a picture. It's all jumbly. Not a bit like it looks on the lid of the box.'

Dee sent him a glance of sympathetic understanding. She knew just how he felt. Her voice encouraged, 'Keep trying. It will all work out as you go along,' while her mind wondered, Will

my picture work out? The picture she had
mapped out for her own future—would it, too,
slot together as she went along?

It had all seemed straightforward to start with.
She had had only two objectives, both of them
simple enough in themselves. She would steer
clear of men. And travel. Simple! Her road had
led straight ahead, the future clearly defined.

Luke had introduced the first twist.

His behaviour last night blurred the outlines,
and jumbled the picture, and Dee hung on grimly
to the scattered pieces, fearful that the memory
of his kisses might destroy her ability to slot them
together into the picture she wanted them to be.

The rest of the day passed more easily than she
had dared to hope, until the time came for herself
and Luke to set out for the airport.

As he bade his friends goodbye Dee heard
Manoj ask, 'Will your parents be home in time
for the exhibition, Luke? It will be nice to see
them again,' and he replied,

'I'm afraid not. Since Dad retired they've taken
to globe-trotting. They are still on the last lap of
their current cruise. They should be back by the
time you come again, though, in the spring.'

'We'll look forward to seeing them then,'
Manoj said, and Gita added with a warm smile,

'And Mari, too?'

'And Mari, too,' Luke said with an echo of the
same smile, and Dee wondered, as she boarded

the helicopter, Who is Mari? What is she in Luke's life?

She remained silent, sitting behind Luke and the pilot, locked in a world of her own thoughts. Luke's life is not my business, nor mine his, she told herself firmly, but the question persisted as she stared with unseeing eyes out of the aircraft cabin to where a veil of thin mist still blurred the outlines on the ground, making them as confused as her thoughts.

She emerged from her reverie with a start when the pilot began to point out the major sights of the approaching city, now clear and distinct below them. Dee gave herself a brisk mental shake. She hadn't realised they were so close.

'Surely that's the temple where we heard the bells? And the market-place where I bought my scarf?' Eagerly she set about identifying from the air the monuments she had visited at ground level, welcoming the distraction to give herself something else to think about.

When they landed she discovered that Delhi had cooled considerably during her absence, but, in contrast to the keener air of the hills, it was still unbearably hot.

'It's stifling,' she gasped, and Luke slanted her a keen look, and consoled,

'You won't have to endure it for long.'

Endure was a fitting description for sharing Luke's company, Dee thought ruefully, and was prepared to forgive Delhi for any shortcomings when her colleague appeared, complete with car, to meet them.

She wouldn't be obliged to spend the rest of the day alone with Luke, after all.

Her colleague drove them first to Dee's hotel to collect the rest of her luggage, and then on to Luke's for the same purpose, and he remained with them during lunch.

This time, Dee noticed, Luke chose a meat dish, but the business lunch atmosphere lacked the shine of that other, earlier occasion, and she had little interest in her surroundings, and even less in her meal.

They ate mostly in silence, the purpose that brought them all together large in the forefront of their minds, but dangerous to discuss in a crowded dining-room, and Dee grasped at the respite to steady her jangled nerves and hoped that her luck would hold when she eventually reached England.

Until now she had managed to put the prospect of her coming work at Ransom Court to the back of her mind. Now it began to loom close, hovering like a storm cloud on her near horizon, and refusing to be ignored.

She wondered if Bill's itinerary would allow her to snatch a day or two to herself first. She sorely needed a break away from Luke, to enable her to gather her poise before she presented herself at Ransom Court.

Dee gave a wry smile. Present herself at court, at the behest of the king of the antique world. Except that she felt more like a sacrificial offering than a débutante.

She was still unsure what dates Bill had finally fixed for the exhibition. Her last conversation with him had ended on the note, 'Don't bother to ring me at base while you're in the hills with Ransom's friends. Just enjoy yourself. I'll get our Delhi contact to telegraph me details of your return flight, and I'll clue you up when you get back.'

The message to Bill would, as usual, be in code so that it did not draw undesirable attention to her return, with her precious cargo in tow. Dee agreed, 'That's fine. I'll wait until then.'

But now the uncertainty tugged at her stretched nerves. She could ask Luke, of course. He would most probably know. But when he had informed her about offering Ransom Court as the venue for the exhibition he had said nothing about dates, and Dee's pride refused to allow her to question him.

'If you're ready, shall we go?'

Her colleague spoke in a voice that was loud enough to make Dee wonder if he had said the same thing before, probably more than once, and she had been too absorbed in her thoughts to hear him. Confused, she pushed them to one side, mumbled, 'I'm ready,' and wondered wearily,

Ready for what? as she followed the two men out to the car.

The pieces which had been needed to complete the exhibit proved to be modern jewellery at its finest, the very best of its kind in workmanship and design, and as Dee gazed at the glittering pile, assembled for their inspection as before, on black velvet, her eyes reflected the sparkle of the gems.

Each piece was infinitely desirable, individually worth a fortune, and far beyond her own reach, but a cat can look at a king, she told herself amusedly.

By her side, Luke murmured, 'Beauty to adorn beauty,' and she cast him a sharp upward glance.

His eyes were fixed on one particular ring in a set of four, and the glint in them betrayed a desire to own it. For Mari? They were women's rings, not men's. It would have to be someone very special, Dee reflected, to warrant such a costly gift.

She had no doubt that Luke could afford it, although in spite of his wealth she couldn't recall having seen him wear any jewellery himself, not even a signet ring.

Perhaps it didn't turn him on personally? It crossed her mind to wonder, What did? The 'what' turned into 'who', and the name Mari floated across her mind. She pushed it away almost fiercely. She wasn't interested in any 'who' in Luke's life, whatever the name, but the question continued to hover like a persistent insect, and she swatted it determinedly with a brisk query to her colleague, 'Do you have a special carrying case for the exhibits to travel in?'

During her travels for Bill she had never before been in charge of anything small enough to be actually carried on her person. Always the artefacts had been of a size, or a quantity, that warranted packaging, and stowing away in the holds of ships or planes, or in the backs of security vans, always accompanied but never carried by Dee personally.

The whole of this consignment put together would fit into a couple of good-sized pockets, most of the space being needed by the antique exhibits. It made the personal risk to the courier who carried the case so much the greater, and was the point of Luke's harsh criticism.

Her colleague nodded. 'It's a small briefcase, with all the usual security devices.'

That meant a chain to lock it to her wrist, with a loud hail alarm, and probably a smoke signal of some kind, activated by a good hard tug at the chain such as a thief might make.

The man reached towards a case standing on the floor under the table, and instantly Luke checked him by a firm, 'It will be safer to do it my way.'

He pulled a soft leather strip from his pocket with strap ends resembling a body belt, and Dee

watched with growing astonishment as he un-
rolled it on to the table, and began calmly to fit
the exhibits into the small pockets cut deep into
the leather, until only the four rings were left still
lying on the table.

When he was satisfied that the items were all
securely enclosed Luke began to strap the filled
belt round his waist, underneath his khaki bush
shirt. A detached part of Dee's mind realised that
this must be why Luke had worn casuals, instead
of a suit, to travel in.

It had surprised her when he had appeared in
mufti at breakfast time. Now the reason became
obvious. Even such a small item as a piece of
jewellery would stick out to spoil the line of the
perfectly fitted tailoring of his cream linen suit,
and so betray the presence of something to hide
to the eyes of those they most wanted to hide it
from.

Something else dawned upon her: Luke had
come ready prepared to collect the gems and carry
them on his own person. Always before, when
clients had provided her with an escort, that
escort had deferred to her decision as to how the
cargo was to be handled.

This escort made his own decisions, and expected her to defer to them. He had not bothered
to consult her beforehand, but had simply gone
ahead and brought the leather belt with him,
taking her acceptance for granted.

Expecting her to fall into line without demur. In tandem. Resentment spilled out of Dee, and she turned on Luke.

'It's my job to carry the exhibits, not yours. I'm the one who is insured. The case will be safer. It will be locked to my wrist.'

'And advertise to any interested parties that we're going home loaded.' Luke continued to buckle, and his words gave Dee pause, checking the explosive protest that sprang to her lips.

'Interested parties' meant international jewel thieves, who would stop at nothing to gain what they wanted. And 'loaded' was right. The jargon of the trade. Laconic, descriptive, totally chilling. Dee felt herself go colder still at Luke's next words.

'You can wear the rings on your fingers.'

She stared at him. '*Wear* them?' She gulped, and had to take a hard breath before she could go on. She felt her mouth to be wide as her eyes with shock, and with an effort she snapped it shut, and gritted, 'You can't be serious. After all you said about Bill being careless of safety, and now you have the nerve to suggest that I actually wear the rings on my fingers? You must be out of your mind. It's inviting trouble to carry the rings in full view.'

'Turn the stones round in your palm, and close your fingers over them. That way only the gold bands will show, and I'll hold your hand to cover those.' A slight smile lifted the corners of Luke's lips. 'Your hand is tiny enough to go right inside mine.'

Dee opened her mouth to protest, and Luke's voice hardened on an authoritative note. 'No one is going to take any notice of a couple holding hands, particularly when they're dressed in holiday gear. They'll think the obvious, and lose interest.'

'Oh, great!' Dee muttered under her breath, and Luke cast her a searching glance.

'If any members of the Press happen to be around when we get to Heathrow, and they get the wrong impression, too bad.'

Too bad for who? For Luke? Or for herself? Or the unknown Mari? Perhaps Luke was giving her, Dee, a warning not to get the wrong impression herself from the fact that they had spent the holiday in the hills together, and that he had kissed her, and now suggested holding hands.

He had no need to worry on that score, she thought hardly. She intended to fit the pieces of her personal jigsaw into a picture of her own choosing, not his.

Whatever his reasons, his logic was unarguable, and Bill would expect her to go along with what he said. Had, indeed, instructed her to do so. There was no dishonour in strategic withdrawal when it was in a common cause. Only dented pride, and an unseemly desire to shout at Luke 'Wear the rings yourself, and hold your own hand'.

With an effort she choked the words back, and reached out towards the glittering display on the table with a hand that shook. She touched the first ring, fumbled, and it rolled away from her fingers, and Luke, watching her closely, said, 'Let me.'

He picked up her left hand in his, and then paused, and his eyes searched her face. Dee realised, dismayed, He's felt the tremble. He said, quietly and without inflexion, 'If you're afraid, I'll carry them myself.'

She was afraid, desperately so, but not of wearing the jewels. Not of jewel thieves, who might try to snatch the gems from her, perhaps causing her physical harm in the process.

What she feared was the electric touch of Luke's fingers over her own, carefully separating one suddenly numb digit from the other, the better to slide on the rings.

She feared—oh, how she feared!—the fire which spread through her veins at his touch, and burned in his curiously flecked eyes as he watched her, waiting for her to reply.

The silence stretched. Luke seemed to have been holding her fingers forever. Dee became vaguely aware of her colleague in the background, watching and waiting too. She drew a deep, steadying breath. Only one. There wasn't time for three. But it was enough to float out the lie between her clenched teeth, 'I'm not afraid.'

Luke nodded as if satisfied, and began to slide the rings on to her fingers. He was a perfectionist. He put on one, and took it off again, repeating the process until he was satisfied that each ring rested on the finger it best fitted.

When all of them nestled safely, he held up her hand as if to satisfy himself that he had fixed them to his liking, and Dee looked on in silence at the galaxy of beauty adorning her fingers, such as they had never done before, and never would again.

They tingled with the warm contact of Luke's grip as he carefully slid each ring into place. One, two, three, four. Her mind counted them automatically. For better, for worse, for richer, for poorer. Why did he have to choose her left hand? Was it a random choice that he had put two of the rings on her engagement finger, one of them the ring that had attracted his special attention?

Hurriedly Dee sent her mind in search of another rhythm to fit. Rich man, poor man, beggar man, thief. That was more appropriate, except that the rich man confronting her threatened also to be the thief, stealing not precious stones, but her own infinitely more precious freedom.

Dee lowered her hand and clenched it convulsively into a fist, turning the stones from view. He must not succeed. Mari, whoever she was, must have no rival.

CHAPTER SIX

LUKE held Dee's hand in the back seat of the car, all the way to the airport.

Just like an ordinary courting couple, she thought with a giggle that died in a gasp of protest as his fingers clamped over her own like steel bands, completely engulfing them, pressing the hard edges of the gems into her flesh with painful force. Chaining her to him. She tried unavailingly to tug her hand free, protesting, 'There's no need for you to hold my hand in the car. No one can see. If *you're* scared,' she lashed him with scorn to try to gain her release, 'I'll sit on my hand and keep it out of sight.'

Anything would be better than the electric impulses flowing from his touch, which set her every nerve-end jangling, not just her fingers.

'I'll hold on to you,' he answered curtly, and did. 'That way I know you'll be safe.'

'*You*'ll be safe'. Not '*the rings* will be safe'. Would he have been so concerned for her safety if it hadn't been for the rings? The answer was obvious, and extinguished the small warmth which had started into life inside her, and she pointed out flatly, 'The car doors are locked.'

'If your training in security was as good as you claim, you must know that locks wouldn't stand a chance against a determined raid.'

Luke always had the last word. With tightened lips Dee turned her head away, and looked out of the car window on her side.

Her eyes widened on a brightly decorated elephant that plodded towards them, urged on by its watchful keeper. It headed a noisy procession of people which took up half the street, obviously celebrating a festival of some kind.

Or on their way to try to wrench open the car door and steal their precious cargo? Were the elephant, and the musicians, and the noise just a front to cover a more sinister purpose?

Locks wouldn't stand a chance against a determined raid...

Dee shrank back against Luke as the animal came closer and forced the car to slow to a crawl in order to allow it to pass.

She felt Luke's hand over her own tense and tighten. Her nerves screwed to screaming pitch as the elephant's huge bulk loomed over the car, the searching trunk investigating the paintwork.

The chains in its keeper's hands were strong enough to remain intact if they were flung through the window, and round the door-jamb, when one good pull by the animal they were attached to would be enough to rip the car in half.

And expose herself and Luke to attack.

Dee flinched away, pressing herself against muscular hardness, reassuring hardness under the khaki bush shirt, feeling the ridge of the leather belt and its contents round the tight waist.

The elephant plodded peacefully past, and the noisy crowd melted along with it, and Dee felt herself go limp. Reaction brought with it anger, and she hated Luke for frightening her unnecessarily. Hated herself for showing fear.

Taking delivery of priceless artefacts was always a nerve-stretching business, bad enough when she merely accompanied the cargo. A thousand times worse, she discovered, when she was actually wearing it. Her escort, who was supposed to take the tension out of the exercise, was deliberately adding to it, she blamed Luke bitterly.

Frightening a female courier was just another way to show his power. Abruptly Dee sat upright, away from him, putting distance between them that was no distance at all because he continued to hold on tightly to her hand.

People, and what they were carrying with them, *could* be snatched from cars. It happened. But mostly in films. This was not a film. This was the real world, the sane world, in which danger was recognised, but rarely happened.

Dee's lips curled in the darkness of the car, and she steeled her fingers to lie limp and unresponsive in their prison. She wouldn't give Luke another opportunity to feed his ego at her expense.

They had remained in the bank for some time, completing the documents necessary to enable them to clear Customs with their cargo, and it was dark when they had finally emerged.

Her colleague had said, 'I'll drive you to the airport in my own car. It's less noticeable than a bank van,' and added, 'I've spoken to Customs, both here and in London. One of their officers will meet you at each end, and steer you through without fuss. It will lessen the risk.'

'Identification?' Luke had asked immediately, and the other man had answered.

'Both of the officers will be known to you personally, Mr Ransom.'

To Luke. Not to Dee. With an effort she had swallowed her frustration and followed the men to the car.

The darkness outside was at once a cover, and an increased risk. To Dee's nervily alert eyes the streets had seemed to be much more crowded than usual. Perhaps because of the festival which had brought out the crowd with the elephant? Festivals in India meant lots of people in the streets, crowding round the traffic, reducing its speed.

A golden opportunity for thieves to attack, and grab, and melt away again afterwards into the crowd, uncaught. The tension returned. Lights flickered in windows, from the flaring of countless candles. Dee turned her eyes enquiringly on to Luke's face, and he answered her unspoken question.

'It's the start of Diwali, the Festival of Light. There will be musicians on the streets, and processions, and fireworks.'

Fireworks? That would account for the bang she had heard the night before. Another piece of the jigsaw slotted into place.

After the heightened tension the sheer normality of the flight came as an anticlimax. The alerted Customs man dealt with their exotic luggage with smooth efficiency, and in a separate room, and then exceeded his duties by insisting they bypass the usual boarding formalities, and escorted them on to the plane himself.

He, too, was well aware of the risk, and didn't want any untoward incident to rebound upon his own head.

As he escorted them to their seats, before leaving them in the care of the stewardess, Dee heard one impatiently waiting passenger grumble discontentedly, 'Money talks,' and another answer, 'More likely to be trouble of some kind. The girl looks as if she might be under arrest. Did you see how the man was holding on to her?'

Arrest was what it felt like, Dee thought ruefully as Luke steered her into the window-seat and sat down next to her, still holding tightly to her hand. He didn't release her until the plane became airborne, and then not before his fingertips had cautiously investigated, to make sure the gems were, as he had instructed, turned round into her palm.

Contrarily, the moment Luke released them Dee's fingers felt bereft.

They straightened with quick longing, flexing themselves to reach out and curl round Luke's hand, and hold their erstwhile protector to them, and, scorning their weakness, Dee sent her other hand to cover them, but, although it held them in submission, it couldn't make up for their lack.

To occupy them she forced them instead to attend to the in-flight meal, cutting food which she didn't want to eat, and raising drink to her lips that, for all her muddled senses were aware, might have been tea, coffee, or river water.

The flight itself proved to be uneventful. The passenger who occupied the third seat, next to Luke, was an expansive middle-aged lady, returning from a package tour and full of her once-in-a-lifetime holiday. Separated from her fellows by the seating arrangements, she turned to Luke and Dee for conversation, and thankfully Dee let her talk, welcoming the distraction to her own unwelcome thoughts.

'It's going to feel cold when we get out at Heathrow after all that lovely sunshine, isn't it?' their fellow traveller prophesied with a shiver. 'I hope you've got something warm on under that nice suit, dear?' Her eyes assessed Dee's neat two-piece with the resigned look which had long since learned to bypass anything under a size sixteen.

Dee hid a smile. 'I've got a light coat with me, if I need it.'

'A coat is all very well.' The tightly permed curls wagged disapprovingly. 'It's underneath you need the warmth. My daughter, now, she's about your age, and she simply refuses to wear a vest.' She sighed resignedly. 'It doesn't matter what I say. And as for the things she wears in bed...' The curls shook again. 'What I say is, she might as well not bother. Nothing but a bit of lace and ribbon, that's all they are. Not enough to keep a body warm. I keep telling her, get yourself some nice winceyette pyjamas. They're the things for cold weather.'

Dee clamped down hard on a rising giggle, and beside her she felt Luke stir. She glanced up quickly and met merriment in his narrowed eyes, and averted her own hastily lest her giggle betray her. Unaware of the exchange, their companion shrugged plump shoulders and complained, 'You youngsters never listen. I don't suppose you've got anything warm either... Oh, duty frees? Yes, please.'

She turned her attention to the hovering stewardess, and Luke leaned down and murmured *sotto voce* in Dee's ear, '*Have* you got any winceyette pyjamas?'

With an effort, Dee kept her face straight. 'As a matter of fact, I have,' she answered primly.

Luke's eyebrows registered his astonishment, and, unable to help herself, Dee let the laughter surface in a gurgle as she confessed in a whisper, 'My grandmother gave them to me for Christmas, years ago. They're bright pink, with big roses all over them. Sensible, she said they were.'

'And?' Luke's dancing eyes hung on her answer, and she grinned.

'They're still in the packet.'

Their arrival at Heathrow was greeted by two bored-looking newspaper reporters, who were waiting for a VIP due on a much delayed flight. 'Haven't seen you around for a while, Mr Ransom,' one of them called out, and Luke answered,

'I've been abroad.'

Dee felt him tense as the two men approached them, and his hand round her own tightened its grip. Luke took no chances, even though he obviously recognised the two men, and Dee noticed that he treated them with the same automatic courtesy that seemed to be a part of him, and brought him willing service where others, more demanding, were forced to wait.

'Business, or pleasure?' one of them asked, with his eyes fixed significantly upon Dee.

'You could say a bit of both,' Luke drawled.

'Did you *have* to say that?' Dee muttered furiously.

It gave the men *carte blanche* to make whatever they liked of the fact that Luke was holding her hand. She stiffened as the reporter's alert glance slid over her, taking in every detail of her appearance. Making mental notes so that he could describe her accurately in his paper's gossip column?

Dee wondered disjointedly which newspaper he represented. Was it one of the rags? It scarcely mattered, since the undergrads at home read a wide selection, most of which found their way, sooner or later, into the hands of her family via their 'daily'.

Dee's only consolation was that the reporters didn't know her name. She could only hope that any description, if it was printed, might go unnoticed at home. If not... Her raw nerves quivered at the prospect of her mother speculating. Of Oliver teasing, reminding her of his bet. Of her sister-in-law saying, 'I told you so.' She wondered what Mari would think if she read it.

At least there wouldn't be a picture to back up the description. Luke never, ever allowed his picture to appear in newspapers.

The reporter begged, 'Be a sport, Mr Ransom. Give us a shot, just this once. If the VIP doesn't arrive, and we don't go back with something, our editor will have us for breakfast.'

'Just this once, then.'

Dee's ears refused to believe what they had heard. Luke didn't...he couldn't...he *had*. '*No!*'

she protested, and shot him a look of urgent appeal, and at that moment the camera clicked.

Luke collected his car from the long-stay car park. It was a low-slung grey Jaguar, sleek and powerful, like its owner. Glowering, Dee got in beside him, and when a short time later they reached base, and Bill approved, 'It was a good move to wear the rings,' she snapped ungraciously,

'It was Luke's idea, not mine.'

One part of Dee's mind registered that, in spite of Luke's earlier, harsh criticism of her boss, the two men appeared now to be on amicable terms, while the other took in Bill's probing look at her use of Luke's first name.

Dee's face became stony. The moment they were alone together she would wipe out the hopeful look on Bill's face, and explain in no uncertain terms exactly what was her relationship with Luke. In the meantime it rankled that her escort should get the credit for doing her job.

Hurriedly she stripped the jewels from her fingers and thrust them into the tray which Bill provided, not without a lingering look at the one particularly attractive ring which Luke, too, had admired, and which had fitted on to her finger as if it belonged there.

Resolutely pulling her eyes away, she slid the tray into the safe Bill had opened to receive it, and Luke reached under his bush shirt and unstrapped the soft leather body belt.

'The rest of the exhibits are in this.'

To Dee's astonishment, Luke handed the belt to her to give to Bill, a token gesture of her responsibility which, she thought sourly, came too late to salvage her pride.

She reached out to take it from him, and immediately she felt the soft leather touch her fingers she wished contrarily that Luke had bypassed her and handed it straight to Bill instead. The belt was still warm from contact with its wearer's body, and her fingers clenched convulsively round it as a wave of sensation flowed from the warmth and set her fingertips burning as if they had received an electric shock.

Hurriedly she released the belt to Bill, dumping it into his outstretched hand with unseemly haste, aware of his startled look. She averted her eyes from Luke's face, shrinking from the derision she knew must be there, that had noticed her haste to rid herself of the burden and guessed its cause, and would prove to be the last straw in a day that had unmercifully piled one on top of the other.

Bill stowed away their cargo and locked the safe with the satisfied comment, 'Those will be all right in there for the next twenty-four hours,' and Dee thought with relief, Twenty-four hours is just what I need to give me space away from Luke.

Space to regain her composure, and the opportunity, when she reached home, to field any newspapers containing the photograph of herself and Luke together before they were able to cause speculation among her family. News of the picture was bound to filter through, in the small, gossipy community, but by the time it did she would be away again on another assignment, out of reach of both questions and teasing, and when she returned the nine days' wonder would have died down and given place to other things.

What the photograph would do to the girl called Mari, if she saw it, was her problem. And Luke's. Dee knew a malicious satisfaction that his outrageous behaviour could rebound upon his own head and leave him with some awkward explanations to make. She said out loud, striving to keep the relief out of her voice, 'Twenty-four hours will give me nice time to go home and sort out my clothes, and collect my car.'

The two men spoke at once. Bill said, 'Betty will collect any clothes you need,' and Luke put in,

'You won't need your car.'

'I must have wheels if I'm to commute between home and Ransom Court.'

Even as she voiced her protest, Dee had the feeling that something was being stacked against her. Luke confirmed her intuition with a masterful, 'You won't be commuting. You'll be living at the court for the duration of the exhibition. It's all arranged.'

Without her consent! Anger and dismay fought for supremacy as Dee sought desperately for a means to extricate herself, when a cheerful voice enquired into the strained silence, 'Did I hear my name mentioned?'

Betty, Bill's indispensable secretary and Jill-of-all-trades, popped her head round the door of her boss's office, and Bill nodded.

'Yes, come in a minute. Dee is going to need clothes collecting from home. Can you do the usual?'

'Of course.' It was a request Betty was well used to from couriers in a hurry. 'Tell me what you want,' she said practically to Dee. 'If I go right away the van driver will be able to deliver your case to Ransom Court almost as soon as you get there yourself.'

'She won't need the pink winceyette pyjamas,' Luke said, pan-faced, and Dee's own face flamed. She didn't know where to look. What to say. She wanted to disappear from view by the quickest possible route. Most of all she wanted to slay Luke.

Betty's eyes popped. Bill scowled, and a dozen questions chased one another across his homely features. The chief one was, had he been right, after all, to accept Luke Ransom's offer?

Dee found her voice. She managed to stammer, 'I haven't... I didn't... I...'

Her voice trailed into silence. She threw Luke a look that should have reduced him to ashes, and, grabbing Betty urgently by the arm, she hissed, 'Let's go into your office. I'll write out the things I need in there.'

Anything to get away from Bill's reproachful gaze and Luke's sardonic look. She stumbled out on legs that didn't seem to belong to her, and when she slammed the outer office door behind them Betty quizzed with a mischievous grin, 'You look as if you need a stiff drink more than clothes right now.'

Dee let out her pent-up breath in a rush. 'Now I know what it feels like to want to commit murder.'

'Start writing your list instead,' Betty advised, and asked interestedly, 'What's all this about pink winceyette pyjamas? I didn't know you had any.'

'It's a long story. I'll tell you some time.' Dee forced her voice to speak normally. 'There's something else I need, more than clothes. More, even, than a stiff drink.' She looked appealingly at Betty. 'When you go home will you try to get hold of Mary?' Mary was their faithful daily, and could be relied upon as an ally in times of stress. 'Ask her to waylay any newspapers,' Dee begged, 'before the family have a chance to get hold of them. Get her to fillet out any with my photograph in them, will you? It won't delay the kill, but at least it will keep the hounds off my trail for a bit longer. I've got enough to handle at the moment with this exhibition, without having to cope with family curiosity on top.'

Any more pressure and she would scream, she promised herself. Out loud she explained to Betty, who laughed, 'Why bother to waylay the photographs? Your mother will be over the moon to see her last unmarried daughter side by side with a world-famous antiques dealer.'

'If she is she'll be the only one,' Dee assured her grimly.

'Why? Most girls wouldn't say no to being photographed with Luke Ransom. You must admit, he's dishy, as well as being rich. It isn't often you get both in one package, and a young one at that.'

'I'm not most girls. I intend to stay solo, so don't run away with any wild ideas.'

'Solo. *So lo*nely,' Betty quipped, only half joking.

Recently divorced, Betty should know. Dee bit back her flippant rejoinder. The secretary's experience merely served to reinforce her own resolution, and to save herself from having to answer she turned her attention to writing the list, but the secretary persisted, 'It's lover-boy out there who might be getting wild ideas, not me.'

'He's *not* lover-boy,' Dee gritted. 'At least, not so far as I'm concerned. And, if he does get any wild ideas, I'll slap them down fast.'

She administered the first verbal slap when she and Luke were *en route* to Ransom Court an hour or so later. 'What on earth made you say such a thing to Betty?' she demanded indignantly.

'What about?'

'You know full well what about. Winceyette pyjamas.'

Luke shrugged. 'It seemed logical. You won't need warm whatnots at Ransom Court, no matter what our chatty passenger said on the plane. My home has full central heating,' he claimed virtuously, with the air of a hotel proprietor advertising five-star facilities.

'Oh, *most* logical,' Dee agreed sarcastically.

That was not his reason, and Luke knew it. He had said it in order to disconcert her, enjoying his power to do so, and it did nothing for her confidence to know that he had, once again, succeeded.

As before, Luke drove in silence, and Dee allowed it to remain unbroken. Not for the first time in his company she felt angry, frustrated, and curiously helpless, with Luke firmly in the driving seat, and herself, as a passenger, obliged to go along with wherever he chose to lead.

He steered the car through the evening traffic build-up with smooth efficiency, decanted it on to the motorway, where its power made light of the miles, and unconsciously Dee began to relax, soothed by the gentle motion of travel, so that when Luke finally turned off on to quiet country lanes, slowed the speed to a gentle cruise, and remarked idly, 'Do you know the Chiltern Hills at all?' it was easier than she'd expected to answer him casually.

'I've only got a passing acquaintance with them.'

The countryside through which they were passing was neutral ground, and she stepped on to it gratefully, glad to give her sorely taxed patience a rest. Getting angry with Luke, she discovered, was as wearing as it was unprofitable. To keep it at bay she enlarged, 'Mostly I've just driven through the Chilterns on my way to somewhere else. It's chair-making country, isn't it? All those beech trees...'

'Famous for them,' Luke confirmed. 'You've come at the best time of the year to explore the area. You should see a little of it while you're here. The colours of the woods are lovely in the autumn.'

With luck, Dee hoped, she would be kept much too busy at the exhibition to have any time to explore. She didn't relish the prospect of Luke acting as her guide. She answered non-committally, 'The colours are magnificent.'

Was it because she had never before caught the beech woods at their moment of peak autumn glory? Or was it because Luke was sitting beside her that each vivid colour seemed to take on an extra glow?

The thought was a warning, and, struggling with its implications, Dee was unprepared for what was to follow. The car breasted a rise, and she felt it slow down. She went rigid. Surely Luke wasn't so corny as to claim to have run out of petrol? She sent him a hostile look, but he remained relaxed in his seat, and merely gestured forward with his hand.

'Ransom Court,' he said.

Dee turned her head, and followed the direction in which he pointed, and didn't answer. For the moment she couldn't. The house lay below them, resting in a fold of the hill, and sheltered by thickly hung beech woods, which were clothed in their fiery autumn garment of orange and yellow and red. Water shimmered, a circle of silver surrounding the house itself.

The dipping sun turned the dying leaves to fire. It glanced off the water, gilded crazily corkscrew chimneys, and rested benignly on old walls, lighting up their skeleton beams, and warmly coloured herringbone-patterned brickwork.

Dee drew in a deep breath of pure pleasure. Ransom Court was a jewel, in a setting of gold. Unexpected tears stung her eyes as they drank in the scene for long moments before, 'How can you bear to go away, to travel so much, and leave all this behind?' she breathed.

The man sitting beside her slanted her a long look, but Dee was too fixated by the scene in front of her to notice. He took some time to frame his answer, and when he did it came in a quiet, reflective tone.

'I suppose because I know it's always here to come back to.'

Dee turned her head then, and met his look, and pulled her eyes away again quickly. So the globe-trotting tycoon was human enough to need a base. A home. She twisted this new piece of the jigsaw round in her mind for a moment or two, and then let it rest there, uncertain as yet where it would fit. It needed another piece to lock into. Mari? Unconsciously she shook her head, as if to shake the name out of her mind, and asked, 'It's Tudor, isn't it?'

'Mostly, with bits of other periods added on here and there. Some of it is even older. Fortunately it came through the war intact.' He grimaced. 'My ancestors would arise in wrath if anyone had suggested using modern materials, like concrete, to repair any damage.'

Ancestors meant generations of the same family living in the same house. Getting married, giving birth, dying. Dee examined the idea dispassionately, surprised to find that it held a curious appeal so far alien to her freedom-loving mind. Perhaps places like Ransom Court did that to you. At least Luke's home was not merely a status symbol, acquired by the *nouveau riche*.

She slotted the piece of jigsaw into place, and wondered about Luke's parents. As if he had read her thoughts, he handed her the next piece unasked.

'These days my parents live in the dower house. After my father retired the court became too large for them, and, as I need space to entertain the occasional client, I took it over. The arrangement works very well.'

Luke needed space, and a suitably exotic setting. His clients were drawn from the wealthy and the influential world-wide, as would be those who attended the coming exhibition.

In spite of herself, Dee felt an urge to learn more about her enigmatic companion, who guarded his privacy so successfully. She despised her own curiosity, but the urge was too strong, and it made her send out a leading, 'It's unusual to see a real moat these days. They have mostly all been drained and filled in.'

'The moat is an added security measure. Basic, but very effective. Even the most dedicated thief hesitates to get his feet wet. When the drawbridge is raised there is no other way into the court.'

The water in the moat was wide, and dark, and deep, and would wet more than the feet of any would-be intruder. Dee gave an involuntary shiver, which was nothing to do with her light clothing, because the car was comfortably warm.

Sheer walls rose from the water, as thick and unscaleable as the barrier which Luke erected round his private life, and which, until the airport photograph, not even the Press had managed to penetrate.

Dee found this glimpse into his inner sanctum both fascinating and disturbing. She stirred restlessly as Luke quit the car and strode towards two strong-looking metal uprights which supported the bridge. He unlocked a control panel in the nearest upright, and manipulated some buttons in what was obviously a pre-arranged code, making it plain that the watery deterrent was merely a back-up to a modern, and highly efficient, electronic security alarm system.

She instinctively ducked, and recovered herself quickly with an embarrassed, 'Silly of me!' as the huge drawbridge began to descend over the water, and Luke smiled as he rejoined her and slid back behind the steering-wheel.

'It usually has that effect upon people the first time.'

Had it had that effect upon Mari?

Dee was left with no time in which to speculate. The drawbridge closed behind them automatically as soon as they reached the other side. And then Luke's hand cupped her elbow, steering her under an impressive coat of arms above a high studded doorway, and into a hall, where a bright log fire burned in a stone grate, and a bowl of chrysanthemums rivalled the vivid colours of the beech trees outside.

A motherly looking middle-aged woman hurried across the hall to meet them. 'It's good to have you home, Mr Luke.'

'It's good to be home, Kate.' Luke folded her in his arms and kissed her with an affection that told Dee that the woman, who she later learned had been Luke's nurse and was now his housekeeper, was no longer a servant, but a valued member of his family.

'I've turned on the heating, like you said,' the housekeeper told him. 'All the bedrooms are nice and warm.'

No need for winceyette pyjamas.

Instant panic struck Dee. Luke could not, *must not* repeat his infamy here, in front of his housekeeper. If he did she would never forgive him. She would walk out, and leave him flat to cope with the exhibition himself, no matter what Bill said.

And then she remembered. The drawbridge was closed, and there was no way back across the moat without it, and she didn't know the combination of buttons to make it work. By pulling up the drawbridge Luke had effectively sealed off any avenue of escape.

She sent him a hunted look, read in his eyes the derision that saw her fear, and jeered at it, and cruelly kept her hanging over a precipice of uncertainty, until Kate pulled her back on to terra firma with a brisk, 'I'll take you up to your room now, miss. Dinner will be in half an hour. I expect you'll be glad to rest after your long journey.' She chatted amiably on the way upstairs. 'Travelling all that way must be exhausting.'

Dee was well used to travelling. The miles did not exhaust her. Holding her own against Luke did.

She explained to Kate about her lack of luggage, and wondered anxiously, 'How will the van driver get in when he comes? The draw-bridge is closed.'

Perhaps, in spite of what Luke had said, there was a back entrance that was kept permanently open? Kate dashed her rising hope with a simple, 'He'll ring the bell.'

Dee's anxiety evaporated on a laugh. 'You make it sound like a suburban semi.'

'Cottage or castle, they all have to be run along the same lines,' the housekeeper returned prac-tically, and opened a door on the wide landing. 'I've put you in this room, miss. You'll find plenty of hanging space for your clothes when your case arrives. Is there anything you need right away?' she asked kindly. 'If not, I'll leave you to freshen up, while I go down and cast my eye on how the dinner is coming along.'

She paused with her hand on the door-knob. 'Oh, by the way, I hope you don't mind—there are a couple of things still left in the one wardrobe. I've had to leave them there because all the other rooms will be occupied by gentle-men, or couples, while the exhibition is running. We've got a full house,' she smiled, 'and I thought, you being a lady on your own...'

Solo. So lonely.

Dee answered, 'Of course I don't mind,' and wondered as she slid her arms out of her coat, and opened the wardrobe door, what secrets it was about to reveal.

Her eyes widened on the sophisticated black lace négligé. Its gossamer delicacy, banded together by ribbon and minuscule pieces of pure silk sewn in at strategic places, dragged an admiring, *'Wow!'* from her lips.

Not enough to keep a body warm...

But, speaking eloquently of that body being young, and lovely, and desirable... Dee grinned. No wonder the housekeeper didn't want it left in one of the other rooms. Its presence was enough to give rise to all sorts of comments and questions. The obvious one tracked across her own mind.

Who owned such diaphanous garments?

Whoever they belonged to obviously loved ribbon and lace. Loved life, and laughter—and love? Luke's love?

Dee's grin faded as she recalled his indulgent smile, the way his stern features had softened when he'd spoken a girl's name.

Mari.

CHAPTER SEVEN

WHERE were all the others?

Where were the gentlemen Kate had mentioned? And the couples who were supposed to be occupying the other bedrooms? The dinner table was laid for two. Dee advanced into the dining-room on feet that suddenly faltered with an urgent desire to turn and run the other way.

Before they had time to put her craven wish into action Luke's tall figure detached itself from the stone balustrade of a balcony leading off the dining-room and overlooking the moat and the darkening sweep of fields and woods beyond.

He strolled towards her, his keen ears alerted to her presence by her light footfall on the parquet flooring.

'Are you cold?' he enquired. 'I'll shut the doors.'

He drew the double french windows to behind him, and Dee allowed the assumption to pass. It suited her to let Luke think it was cold, and not nerves, that caused her involuntary shiver.

She made a small indication towards the table with her hand. 'I thought there would be more of us. Kate said——'

'The others aren't coming until tomorrow. A day before the exhibition opens is all they should need to set up their stands.'

If a day was all that Luke considered necessary for the others, why not for herself? Why did he have to drag her here on a flimsy pretext, denying her the respite she so sorely needed? Her legs folded obediently as he drew out a chair for her at the table, glad to abandon their duties, and Dee viewed the prospect of the coming evening with Luke with growing dismay.

Could she, even now, make some excuse to go back with the van driver when he came, and return with the other people in the morning? Then there would be lots of company. Safe, reassuring company, to take off the edge of Luke's disturbing charisma, the more potent because she was under his roof, in his home, and knew that there was no escape.

Her mind sought for an excuse and failed, as it had done before, to find one that would sound plausible enough to satisfy her host, and, feeling trapped, she turned her reluctant attention to the meal.

Kate bustled in and out, serving dishes that would have done credit to a West End chef, but Dee was in no mood to appreciate food. The housekeeper tut-tutted over her small helpings.

'You're not eating enough to keep a bird alive. You need more than that after a long day of travelling.'

'I'll get my appetite back by tomorrow. I'm too tired now. Although the food is delicious.'

Dee hoped silently that her excuse would serve to remove her from Luke's company the moment the meal was over. In the presence of his housekeeper he kept the conversation general, talking easily about the attractions of the surrounding area.

'We must visit Abinger Hammer. You'll like the village, and the children will enjoy seeing the clock with the figure of the smith on it.'

The moonlit scene beyond the balcony lured them outside after the meal was over. 'Will you be warm enough?' Luke enquired, and Dee answered, 'I'll put on my jacket,' reluctant to miss out on this panacea for her jangled nerves.

Weariness was no longer just an excuse. It homed in on her, a drug disarming her defences, and she leaned her arms along the parapet with a sigh, and gazed down into the quiet water below.

Luke came to lean beside her and she tensed, but, although he came close, their arms did not touch, and she relaxed again. Stone did not conduct electricity, she thought without humour, and fixed her attention on a pair of swans that drifted below them, gliding by with scarcely a ripple towards a thick bed of reeds, which offered them shelter for the night.

Luke followed her gaze, and remarked, 'The same pair stay with us year after year. Some of their young ones go off to make their homes on the bigger lake in the park, but, although they're quite wild, these two seem to prefer to stay on the moat.'

So wild. So free. And yet choosing always to remain in the one place.

Luke added, 'They've been here for so long that they've become part of the scenery. They're always together.'

'In tandem?' Dee enquired drily.

It came out more sharply than she had intended, and Luke turned and regarded her through narrowed eyes that did not pretend to misunderstand her meaning. He answered with a flat, 'They're not fettered. There's no chain binding them together.'

Only the wish.

Dee kept her eyes studiously fixed on the majestic birds below, not meeting Luke's look. No fetters. No chain. Each bird had wings that could lift it far away to explore any corner of the earth. And yet the pair remained tied by an invisible link, the pen swimming meekly behind the cob, content to accept the age-old order of things.

Dee stirred with quick impatience. Such subservience was all very well for swans. She could feel Luke's eyes resting on her face, probing her thoughts, and she pulled her expression into an uncommunicative blank, behind which her mind wondered, Did Luke mind being chained by birth to the home of his ancestors? Did he never want to break free? Or was Ransom Court the anchor that he could put down whenever he wanted to run for harbour, to recharge his personal batteries?

By what means did he recharge them? For a man with his exceptional mind, sport must be only one of many answers. The world knew of his occupation, but nothing of the man himself. Of what he thought, how he felt, and what were his own, very private, dreams. Did he ever let his own personal drawbridge down, and, if so, to whom?

Dee did not know.

As a defence against wanting to, she resolutely turned her mind to the purpose of her visit to Ransom Court, and steered the conversation, and her thoughts, into safer channels with, 'Where exactly in the house are you holding the exhibition?'

'In the main hall.' To her relief, Luke followed her lead. 'It runs along the whole of the one wing. Normally I keep it divided into three rooms with sliding screens, but they can be pushed back if necessary to form one big room.'

One very big room, from the sound of it, which confirmed Dee's impression of the size of the house itself. She asked, borrowing Luke's own earlier brevity on the same subject, 'Security?'

'More than adequate. Apart from Bill Williams's security team, whom you must already know, each individual firm is providing its own selected staff, who will be staying at the court, and will be the eyes and ears for their own exhibits.'

Doubtless the people who would be occupying the other bedrooms. The people she had expected to meet at dinner tonight. Luke went on, 'The exhibits we brought back from India will be attended by staff from one of the international jewellers at this end. My own personal responsibility is for the overall security of the court itself, which is well taken care of by the present alarm system. Which means I shall be able to take time off to show the children round,' he smiled.

Dee said carefully, 'With all those people here to look after the exhibits, why do you need me as well?'

It didn't make sense. Nothing did any more, she decided nervily, and Luke answered, 'I need help to keep balls rolling among the visitors. Bill Williams told me you're used to mixing among people from widely differing cultures.'

'Only university students.'

'Students or adults, it helps when they all come together if there's someone around who is sensitive to their various taboos, and is able to smooth over any difficulties.'

A hostess, in fact. And Luke had no wife to do the job for him.

The explanation hit Dee like a blow. Doubtless Luke's parents would have come to the rescue, but they were still somewhere on the high seas, enjoying their cruise. Manoj and Gita might have helped, but for a good deal of their time they would be in London, only returning to the court during the evening.

Which left herself as a handy substitute. Dee's lips took on a bitter twist. How convenient for Luke that she should be available to be used. She slotted in yet another piece of jigsaw, and fought down an irrational feeling of let-down.

She would like the village of Abinger Hammer, Luke had said. Nice of him to include the hired help in the outing. He cut across her thoughts with, 'You won't need to concern yourself with the sheikh. He will bring his own entourage.'

'*Entourage?*' Dee echoed, her eyes widening.

Luke inclined his head. 'He always travels with a bodyguard.'

Dee grimaced. 'It can't be worth it.'

'What can't be worth what?'

'Being so fabulously rich. What's the use if you have to hire bodyguards to protect you? It's too high a price to pay. His wealth must be a ball and chain to him. He would never, ever feel free.'

'Does being free mean so much to you?'

There was an odd timbre in Luke's voice which arrested Dee's attention, and she turned a wide stare in his direction, but the moonlight that gilded the bronze of his hair left his face in shadow, and she couldn't read his expression.

She had her own reasons for wanting to remain free, which Luke knew nothing about. Silence made a barrier between them, and she bit her lip, unwilling to break it, hiding her innermost feelings from this man who was still, to all intents and purposes, a stranger to her.

A stranger who held a frightening attraction which threatened to undermine her resolution, and if she was so foolish as to allow herself to fall into the same snare again she knew that she would later have to come to terms with the consequences, and pay the price in tears when she moved on and left her heart behind.

That was a secret which Luke must never learn.

It came to Dee that this was the first time since she had met him that she and Luke had been in danger of the kind of personal conversation which enabled people to learn about each other, to go deeper than surface exchanges, and probe into minds and hearts.

With a man of Luke's quick perception she would need to be constantly on her guard if she was to hold on to her secret.

She longed for Manoj and Gita, or the children. Even for the polo pony, which as a last resort she could spur on ahead to avoid having to reply. Always before there had been an escape route, except in the car when Luke had taken her back to her hotel in Delhi, and the time on the bungalow veranda in the hills.

Then Luke had not troubled to talk. He had acted instead. But kisses were not conversation. They spoke a different language, on a subject which needed no words.

To her cost, she had already learned a smattering of that language, but since Alan she had deliberately avoided learning more, since fluency meant commitment. Luke, she discovered, was very fluent.

Did that mean that he was committed?

The question tracked across her mind, even as he drew her into his arms, and then sensation drowned thought as he took her deep into the mysteries of the language that had no words.

His arms held her imprisoned, while his lips opened windows on to other worlds and the kind of commitment which people like Alan would never know. Dee trembled at the view, hating Luke for his slow, mocking smile that witnessed her temptation, confident that he could make her succumb if he really set out to try. Despair claimed her as she felt her resolve begin to weaken, and she strained away from the fierce heat of his exploring lips.

'I'll just clear these crocks away. Is there anything else you need tonight, Mr Luke?'

Kate!

Dee surfaced with a gasp, and couldn't decide whether the housekeeper was friend or foe as Luke's arms dropped to his sides, releasing her, leaving her body contrarily aching for their bondage, and her lips mutely crying out for the pressure of his kiss, while he replied easily, 'Nothing more tonight, Kate, thank you.'

Nothing more tonight... There was more. Much, much more. A new, uncharted world, which beckoned with a siren song in a wild, sweet language that Dee realised now she was only just beginning to learn. She made a small, strangled sound in the base of her throat that the housekeeper must have heard and misinterpreted, because she said with a smile, as if she was answering Dee, 'Goodnight, miss. Sleep well.'

It was the escape route Dee needed. With an immense effort that gave a desperate energy to her trembling limbs, she gathered together the remnants of her self-control, distributed a mumbled, 'Goodnight,' between Luke and his housekeeper, and fled for the sanctuary of her room.

When she reached it her suitcase had been placed neatly on the stand at the foot of her bed. No hope of going back with the van driver tonight.

Shaken, and shaking, she collapsed on to the bed, and lay with her eyes staring up unseeingly at the dark space of the ceiling, which became filled with vivid images of Luke's face, Luke's smile, Luke's laughter, and were joined, like the proverbial skeleton in the cupboard, by a vision of the black lace négligé, hanging in the wardrobe close by, that seemed blacker than the night itself.

Morning brought activity, and people. Blessed people, who bustled round her, giving her no time in which to brood as they drew her willy-nilly into the organised chaos that setting up an exhibition entailed.

It was all new to Dee, the essential follow-on from her own work that hitherto had remained a closed book to her. She opened it gratefully. Setting up an exhibition was the perfect antidote to thinking, she decided, and threw herself energetically into the bustle.

Luke seemed to be everywhere at once, making decisions, ironing out problems, and when they did happen to coincide there was someone else present to lessen the impact.

Burly, competent men set up wooden stands, Bill's team of erectors, who recognised Dee and called out cheerful good-mornings, which lightened her spirits and gave the other exhibition staff an entirely false impression of her status, elevating her in their minds to Luke's second-in-command, and privy to the reasons behind his planning of the lay-out.

Just the opposite was true, she thought ruefully, deftly disposing of a couple of wheres and whats, only to turn and find another exhibitor at her elbow, complaining bitterly about the siting of his stand.

'It's right at the end of the room, the furthest from the door,' he grumbled.

Dee gave an inward sigh and, grasping at inspiration to guide her, she drew the man to one side. In a conspiratorial tone, she soothed his discontented, 'I've been pushed right away in a corner,' with a convincing,

'It's a rather special corner, actually. Mr Ransom works on the theory of leaving the best until the last. You know he has a personal interest in porcelain, and he thinks yours is unique.'

Unique was the kindest description she could think of. Dee hurried on, trying not to allow her aversion for the ultra-modern pottery to show, 'The sun strikes through the stained-glass windows just at this point.' She ad-libbed wildly, and prayed that the windows didn't face north. 'The light falling through the coloured glass will have a charming effect on your exhibits. Visitors will pass by the other stands first, and then come to yours, and notice the difference.'

They would be very short-sighted not to, she thought drily. Ugliness under the guise of art would be truer, if less tactful. She wondered if this was the reason why Luke had tucked this particular exhibitor in an out-of-the-way alcove, and ended rather lamely, 'I'm sure you'll find people will want to stop and buy when they see what you have to offer.'

I sound like an ice-cream seller, she thought with an inward giggle, astonished at her own powers of invention, and equally astonished when the man accepted her explanation with a pleased, 'I hadn't looked at it in that way.'

'Neither had I,' an amused voice confessed in her ear as the potter went back to his stand with a satisfied smile, and Dee spun round and collided with Luke. He put out a hand to steady her, and in the middle of the hustle and the flurry she went deathly still.

Luke's hand held them together, turning them into an island in the middle of a sea of people, whose noisy chatter receded, and left them marooned in a speaking silence, like the void at the eye of a storm.

Luke's words dropped into it, pebbles into a pool, and sent a tremble spreading through Dee in ever-widening ripples as each one hit the surface of her consciousness.

'Keep it up. You're doing a grand job. If it's of any help, the sun *does* shine through that particular window. It faces west.'

It did not help. The information scarcely registered. Only the numbness of 'You're doing a grand job'.

The hired hand, being given a patronising pat on the back for doing a good job that would, no doubt, have been done even better, and as her right, by the owner of the black lace négligé if she hadn't been—where?

Luke laughed down at her, waiting for her to laugh too, but Dee felt as if her face muscles were frozen, while her eyes looked inwards on to a bleak, sunless landscape that stretched endlessly into a footloose and solitary future, and held none of the warmth and bright promise of her dreams.

Solo. So lonely.

The length of snowy white damask tablecloth reflected the ice inside her as she took her place that evening at the dining table, grateful for the twenty or so guests to provide a welcome distraction, and wishing she could have sat among them at the side of the table instead of at the foot, to where Luke had led her, opposite his own seat at its head.

Each time she glanced up his eyes made contact with her own, levelled along the table at her with an all-seeing look that made her concentration waver, so that she lost the thread of what her right-hand neighbour was telling her, and he had to repeat himself before she managed to break the spell of the glowing quartz flecks that mesmerised her power of thought.

'Oh—er—yes, of course,' she managed distractedly.

Her companion smiled. 'Don't you mean, "no"?'

'Do I?' Dee jerked back to what he was saying. 'I'm sorry, I . . .'

'I shouldn't tease,' he remarked contritely. 'You look pale. Are you feeling all right, Miss Tredinnick?'

Pale was how she felt. White. Icy. Frozen inside. She excused her distraction, 'It's been a long day. I only flew in from abroad yesterday. I'm still a bit jet lagged.'

If she kept on like this she would qualify as a writer of fiction. She was becoming adept at invention. Her excuse seemed to satisfy her companion, however.

'Try to get a good night's sleep,' he urged her kindly. 'You'll have an even busier day tomorrow.'

She had received the same advice before, she remembered wryly, and now, as then, she found it impossible to follow, but the exhibitor's prophesy proved to be accurate enough the following day.

As a top-of-the-market exhibition, it didn't attract the huge crowds who attended the usual craft fairs, but by mid-morning the courtyard was filled to capacity with cars, large, luxurious limousines from the world's premier manufacturers and, for the most part, chauffeur-driven.

Watching them arrive, Dee wondered how many of the uniformed figures were bodyguards in disguise, and watched the cars disgorge their owners without envy.

The Arab sheikh arrived with his entourage in two cars. Dee studied the party of robed visitors as they entered the hall with quickened interest. Luke paused beside her on his way to greet them.

'The one in the middle is the sheikh,' he said.

The man was tall, about Luke's height, and handsome in a hawk-like way, with a haughty, aloof expression and ever-watchful eyes, as were those of his companions. The party advanced, and Luke took Dee by the elbow, and drew her forward.

'Come and meet them.'

'Me?' She tried to pull away.

'Of course you.' There was a touch of asperity in his tone. 'That's what you're here for, isn't it?'

Dee no longer felt sure what she was here for. She only knew that it had been a dreadful mistake to come. She felt tense with nerves. What kind of impression would it give to these men to see her by Luke's side, welcoming them into Luke's home, living the lie that she was a bona fide hostess instead of merely a hired help?

Whatever impression its owner received, the hawk face confronting her gave nothing away. The two men greeted each other as old friends, equal in power in their own separate worlds, and a million miles away from her own, Dee thought silently, and then Luke said, 'And this is Dee.'

He gave no further explanation, and Dee's eyes flew apprehensively to the keen, bronzed face above her, and found herself enveloped in a smile of surprising gentleness.

It melted her nerves, and turned the aloof, intimidating, oil-rich man of the desert into a friendly human being, and she realised with a sense of shock, Luke's world is not so very different from mine, after all. Young high fliers, studying at university, or their more mature counterparts, were still people, behind the outward shell.

She smiled back, returning the sheikh's greeting, and did not know how winsome she looked, a tiny figure dwarfed between the two men.

'He's nice,' she enthused to Luke as the entourage moved away to view the exhibits after exchanging a few polite words. 'I hope he finds something he likes among the stalls.'

'He isn't here to indulge himself.'

'Who, then?'

Her upturned face asked the question, and Luke answered it with, 'He's setting up a public museum in his capital city. He was coming to London on a diplomatic mission, so he took time off to come here to see if there was anything suitable to add to what he already has. And to meet Manoj, of course.'

'Manoj?' In the bustle of the morning Dee had temporarily forgotten that the specialist and his family were due at any moment.

'The sheikh wants Manoj to do a similar lecture tour over in his own country. Thanks to his wealth, he has got the ability to build and staff some of the finest health centres that money can buy, and a medical school to back them up.

Which is where Manoj's specialist knowledge will come in.'

'You seem to know a lot about the sheikh.'

'We were all at school together—he, and Manoj and I,' Luke said simply. 'I know him to be a very caring man, with a passionate interest in the welfare of his people. To him, his wealth is merely a means to an end.'

And a burden to be carried for the sake of his people. Dee's gaze followed the man walking in the middle of his ever-watchful bodyguards with a new understanding. Dee turned back to the rest of the exhibition hall, where she was hailed by one of the stand erectors.

'I forgot to give you this.' He thrust a folded newspaper into her hand. 'I thought you probably wouldn't have the time to go out and buy a copy while you were here. It seemed a shame for you to miss it, so I got an extra one, and brought it down with me. Nice picture of you and Mr Ransom, isn't it?'

Dee shook open the newspaper, and stared down at the photograph on the front page with a sinking heart. It was a full-length picture, with a caption that made her cringe: 'Well-known antiques dealer returns home from his latest treasure-hunting expedition.'

Implying that, this time, she might be the treasure.

'*Yuk!*' Dee exploded, and the stand erector grinned.

'They say cameras don't lie,' he teased.

'This one has,' Dee replied forcefully. The camera had caught her gazing up into Luke's face with an expression on her own that suggested she was in the throes of a bad attack of calf love, she thought disgustedly.

Her companion increased her dismay by adding, 'I gave Oliver a copy, too. He thought it was great.'

'Oh, no!' Dee groaned as the man tacked on an afterthought, 'Oliver asked me to remind you about that bet he had with you.'

'What bet was that?' Luke strolled up to join them in time to hear the stand erector's last remark, and there was a distinct edge to his voice as he added, 'And who is Oliver?'

CHAPTER EIGHT

DEE gabbled some excuse, and fled.

One thought was uppermost in her mind. She must get away before Luke saw the photograph in the newspaper. She couldn't bear to look upon his derisive grin when he saw her besotted expression in that awful picture.

It wouldn't matter if he saw it after the exhibition was over and she was gone. She would be spared the embarrassment. She crumpled the offending paper in convulsive fingers, hiding the front page from sight, and behind her she heard both the men start to speak at once.

The erector said, 'Oliver's her... I say, sir, have a care! You've overloaded your stand on this side. It's going to tip—here, let me...'

Luke called out, 'Dee, wait a minute. I want to speak to...'

Dee didn't wait to find out what it was Luke wanted to speak to her about. She dodged among the stalls, seeking to lose herself amid the crowd thronging the aisles in between.

She gave a hunted look across her shoulder. Luke was picking his way steadily among the crowd of visitors, heading purposefully in her direction, and she glanced about her desperately, searching for an avenue of escape.

No doubt the stand erector had already explained who Oliver was. She had no intention of staying around to explain about her brother's silly bet. Nor to give Luke the opportunity to see the newspaper.

The popular daily seemed to burn a hole in her hand. She gave a quick sigh of relief when a visitor waylaid Luke, obliging him to abandon his pursuit for the moment, and Dee looked about her, searching for a means to dispose of the paper somewhere—anywhere—where Luke would not be able to get hold of it.

A set of tall pottery water jars on the nearest stand offered a hiding-place, but the ever-watchful staff were guarding their precious ceramics with eagle eyes, and would make a fuss if she used them as a waste-bin, and would draw even more attention to the very thing she wanted to hide.

A wicker basket caught her eye at the end of the aisle between the stalls, and she headed towards it purposefully, but when she reached it for some reason her fingers refused to let go of the paper.

She gave a furtive look behind her. Luke was once more heading in her direction, and if he saw her drop the paper it would arouse his curiosity even further, tempting him to retrieve it in order

to find out what it was she was so eager to get
rid of.

Excuses for her rebellious fingers flitted
through her mind, none of them convincing, all
of them successful in keeping the newspaper
firmly in their grasp.

I'll find somewhere else. Somewhere safer, she
promised herself, and hated the next unwanted
thought, which suggested, Like the suitcase in
your room?

That would be by far the safest, she mentally
defended her climb-down. It was somewhere that
Luke could not go. She closed her mind to the
next thought, which jeered, Admit it! You don't
really want to throw away the newspaper. You
want to keep the photograph.

She was prepared to admit nothing, least of all
to herself, and, by dint of some avoiding tactics
which would have done credit to an army ma-
noeuvre, she reached her room and buried the
newspaper safely in the depths of her much-
travelled suitcase, and returned to the exhibition
with slightly more confidence.

Not enough for her to want to be alone with
Luke, however. During the hours that followed
her ingenuity was stretched to the limit to keep
him at a safe distance.

His, 'Dee, I want to speak to you privately,'
gradually turned to an exasperated, 'Dee, I *must*
speak to you,' but when he did catch up with her

Dee managed to make sure that somebody else was there as well, preventing any possibility of private conversation.

At dinner that night Luke glowered his frustration at her from his seat at the head of the table, but his words perforce had to remain unsaid.

What could they be about? Dee wondered.

No doubt the stand erector had already told Luke who Oliver was. Not that it was any of his business anyway. And somebody else's wager could hardly be of such importance to make Luke pursue her so relentlessly.

Which left only the newspaper photograph.

Perhaps her panic had been unnecessary, and Luke had already seen the photograph after all? Dee frowned. Did he imagine that she had been playing to the gallery when the newspaper photographer had caught her looking up into his face, with *that expression* on her own?

Did he think—heaven forbid!—that she was trying to compromise him by publicly feigning an understanding between them which did not exist? That her independent stance was merely a front to cover a deeper design? Wealthy men were a prey to such unscrupulous tactics, she knew.

But not—definitely not—by her.

The more Dee thought about it, the more convinced she became that this must be the only explanation for Luke's insistence upon speaking to her in private, to force her to publicly deny any claim on him which the newspaper photograph might imply.

There could be no other subject between them that would demand a tête-à-tête. And there was no other subject of discussion in which she felt less inclined to take part.

With a sinking heart Dee realised that it could only be a matter of time before Luke caught her on her own, but the longer she could manage to delay the confrontation, the better able she would be to face his anger with confidence, when it finally erupted, and deny not only any claim on him, but the remotest desire for one.

Manoj arrived the next day with his family. The perfect antidote to a tête-à-tête, Dee thought gratefully, and resisted Gita's attempts to quieten her two excited sons, who were bursting to tell Dee all about their journey from Delhi.

'I finished my jigsaw puzzle before we came away,' one of the boys told her proudly, and was echoed by his brother,

'And me. Well, nearly.'

Dee thought ruefully, My jigsaw is still in pieces, and none of them seems to fit. But at least the children kept Luke at bay for a little while longer, and after they were in bed that evening Dee and Luke accompanied the boys' parents on a private viewing of the exhibition.

Chatting desperately in order to keep Gita by her side, Dee recounted her difficulty with the stall holder and raised a general laugh, and Gita observed, 'With pottery like that, no wonder he hasn't sold any. I don't like this ultra-modern work myself. It looks dramatic, but it's difficult to live with. I noticed that several of the rings have been sold from the display of Indian jewellery,' she added with evident satisfaction.

One of the first rings to have been sold was the one which Luke had particularly admired. The one Dee herself had liked, which Luke had carefully fitted, with its fellow, on to her engagement finger for safe keeping. Unconsciously the fingers of Dee's other hand rose to rub the now barren member, and she wondered, Was it Luke who bought the ring?

For Mari?

Her hand stilled, and a bleak feeling, as cold as her suddenly nerveless fingers, clutched at her. It hurt, she discovered, to think of another woman wearing the ring which she had worn first. Which was a totally illogical feeling for a self-confessed career woman, but she couldn't help it.

Exasperated with her own confused thinking, Dee flung herself into the visit to Abinger Hammer with a brittle gaiety which kept her thoughts at bay.

Luke took them to see the famous clock, and then drove them to Box Hill afterwards to walk off a superb lunch. The children ran gleefully across the heathland, vying with each other as to which one would reach the top of the hill first, while the grown-ups climbed behind them at a steadier pace.

They reached a particularly steep part, and the men held out their hands to the girls to help them along, Manoj to his wife, and Luke to Dee.

'I can manage.' She tried to step out of his reach, but authoritatively Luke's hand closed over her own, and she couldn't pull away without causing a fuss, although she winced at the strength of his grip.

His fingers round her own were hard and angry, and warned her that they wouldn't let her go until she had heard what it was he wanted to say.

Quick as a thought, Dee reached out her other hand and linked with Gita, foiling Luke's intention to pull her to one side in order to speak to her out of earshot of the others.

'Let's make a line,' she called desperately, coaxing the two children to turn the four into six, making it into a fun thing, and swinging hands as they walked, as children did, joking to hide her fear.

'Phoo, I'm puffed,' she gasped when they finally reached the top of the hill. 'I could have done with a bit more energy to get me up that last bit.'

Gita gave her a sidelong look. 'You should have eaten all your lunch. You left a lot of it. Don't you like stuffed olives?'

'They're not my favourite food,' Dee excused her abandoned meal, shamelessly slandering the chef's exotic creation, and beside her Luke said, in a tone which was as sharp as when he had used the name before,

'Perhaps she prefers Oliver.'

Dee's eyes widened. Whatever was upsetting him, Luke needed not take it out on Oliver. The two had never met. A sharp retort rose to her lips, but Gita forestalled it with a delighted exclamation.

'What a lovely view!'

The countryside opened out in front of them like a map, and they stood to gaze, the two boys demanding Luke's attention to identify recognised spots in the landscape.

It meant he had to loose Dee's hand in order to point out landmarks, and the tense moment passed, and, guarding against its return, Dee attached herself firmly to Gita's side when they turned to walk back downhill.

'Have you two quarrelled?' Gita asked quietly as they followed behind the two men.

'No, of course not. We don't know one another well enough to quarrel.'

The flippancy hid the hurt, but some of it must have showed because Gita sent her a speculative look, and murmured something that sounded like, 'A pity.'

'Dee, what do you call these?' The boys raced up to ask the name of a clump of bright golden wild flowers growing in the grass near by.

'Wild vetch,' Dee answered automatically, while her mind wondered, Why should Gita consider it a pity that she and Luke hadn't quarrelled?

If the older woman only knew, the brooding conflict was about to erupt between herself and Luke the moment they were alone together, and although the autumn sunshine was pleasantly warm Dee felt a shiver pass over her at the prospect of the threatening storm.

Luke's darkening scowl warned her that if she continued to evade him for much longer he would somehow force the issue to get her on her own, and her nerves were on a raw edge as the little party set out to join the local team on the village cricket pitch the next day.

Luke's attempt to walk beside Dee, and draw her out of earshot of the others as they made their way along a winding path through the beech woods, was effectively thwarted by the children's demands to know the history of the cricket team's successes, and when they finally reached the pitch

Dee's fervent prayer was answered by the captain of the team inviting Luke and Manoj to play.

'Your turn will come,' he smiled kindly at the two envious boys. 'Watch us from the stand, and learn from our mistakes.'

Would that she could learn from her own, Dee groaned inwardly. Since she had started on her coveted trip to India her hopes of finding fulfilment in travelling had gone sadly awry, leaving her mind in a turmoil and lost to all previous sense of direction.

She forced her mind to concentrate on the game going on in front of her, and refused to allow herself to think beyond it, occupying herself with picking out the figures of Luke and Manoj among the white-flannelled players.

'Oh, well caught!' She joined enthusiastically in the clapping as Luke expertly fielded a fast ball, and sent the opposing batsman disconsolately back to the stand.

'I do believe you're becoming a cricket fan too,' Gita teased, and Dee shrugged and hoped her rising colour did not show.

'It's more interesting to follow when you know a bit about the game,' she answered offhandedly. 'The boys have been coaching me on the finer points.'

Her interest stemmed from knowing one of the players. Dee tried in vain to thrust down a quick uprush of pride in Luke's neat catch. The palms of her hands stung from the force of her clapping, and she became aware of Gita's amused look, and thrust them under her on the hard wooden bench seat, lest they should be tempted to betray her again.

What on earth is the matter with me? she wondered bewilderedly. If I go on like this I'll be playing cricket myself next.

One small spectator evidently wanted to. An urgent command rose from the pavilion, 'Bundle, come back! Come back here at once.'

The mongrel terrier pretended to be deaf. Balls were something it understood, and it trotted out on to the pitch, determined to join in the fun.

'That's just typical of village cricket.' The dog's owner joined in the general laughter as the game was brought to a halt while the terrier was rounded up and returned to the stand. 'The last time it was a swan that decided to walk across the pitch with a family of cygnets. I must say, Bundle was less trouble to retrieve. The cygnets gave us a merry chase.'

'You're a bad dog,' Dee scolded, smiling, and asked Gita as she fondled the culprit's ears, 'Did your friends get their dog back from the bungalow?'

'What dog?'

'The one that was in the shrubbery the last night Luke and I were there with you. The boys said they had been playing with a dog at their friends' house.'

'That wasn't a real dog. It was only a toy.'

'They said it squeaked.'

'So it does.' Gita's eyes twinkled. 'It drives their parents mad. It's one of those mechanical toys that winds up, and it moves about and squeaks at the same time. Their mother is beginning to wish she had never bought it.'

'I thought the boys meant a real dog.'

'No, although they would love one as a pet. But Manoj won't hear of it. Living in India, the danger of rabies is too great. If we ever go to live abroad perhaps...'

'Rabies?' Cold dread settled like a fog in the pit of Dee's stomach as she remembered, 'Luke said your neighbour telephoned about a dog.'

Gita nodded. 'That's right. He did telephone, to let us know that there was a dog on the loose locally, which was showing suspicious symptoms. It had, in fact, got rabies. We discovered that later, when the bungalow warden shot it in the shrubbery, and put it out of its misery.'

That was the true explanation for the explosion she had heard that night. Not a car backfiring, or a firework. Quite suddenly all the pieces of Dee's jigsaw slotted themselves into place, and she saw the picture clearly for the first time, with all the confusion gone.

She saw the road she really wanted to travel, when it was too late for her to follow it. A deep-seated pain settled in the region of her heart, and grew to unbearable proportions when Gita added quietly, 'That was why Luke raced out into the garden and carried you indoors. He heard the dog whine, and guessed what was the matter. He had encountered rabies before. When we got back to the veranda, after I had checked on the boys, and Luke saw you in the garden, going towards the shrubbery, I have never seen him look so frightened.'

The fear that gripped Dee equalled any that Luke might have felt. She said faintly, 'He didn't tell me the dog had rabies.'

'He wasn't absolutely certain then. He only suspected. It wasn't confirmed until afterwards, and he didn't want to cause you unnecessary alarm.'

Dee felt beyond alarm. She felt absolutely terrified. Far from avoiding Luke, she now wanted to speak to him with an urgency which would not be denied.

She could never afterwards remember how she lived through the next couple of hours. Endlessly long hours, in which she chatted with the cricketers' wives and girlfriends, feigning interest in a game that seemed to go on forever, behaving outwardly as if everything was normal, while inside she twisted in torment.

At last even the players were forced to abandon their game in favour of sandwiches and cakes and cups of tea in the small pavilion, and the torture grew worse as the members of the team resurrected what, Dee thought with frantic impatience, must be every single ball that had been bowled or batted that afternoon, and then some, urged on by the two children who drank in the players' every word with open hero worship.

At last it was over. Dee felt sick and shaking as she joined in the general goodbyes, and wondered how it was that people were still able to act normally when they felt as if they were dying inside.

She was silent as she walked beside Luke when they all set off together through the beech woods, back towards Ransom Court. The trees closed round them as the footpath narrowed, and the children ran on ahead, gleefully kicking up leaves that lay like a flame-coloured carpet on the wood floor.

The path twisted round a clump of huge beech trees, the ancient boles wide and massive, effectively hiding Manoj and his family from sight as they strolled on in front.

Now was her chance!

Dee stopped dead, and spun to face Luke. She reached up and gripped him by both arms to stop him too, and her eyes were anguished pools in her chalk-white face.

'Luke, wait a moment, please. I must speak to you.'

She was conscious of his surprise. Careless of what he thought of her volte-face. She had to know how he felt. How he was. How he would be, for whatever time it took to be sure.

The dipping sun cast Luke's shadow across the golden leaves, darkening them in a long finger pointing along the path. Pointing to where? To what?

Momentarily Dee closed her eyes as the strain of not knowing got the better of her, bringing with it a vision of the rabid dog, lunging forward, snapping at Luke's legs as he swung her high up in his arms, out of reach of danger.

Endangering himself. Risking a hideous disease, and an unthinkable death, in order to keep her safe.

To be loved like that...

She had to know. The words stumbled haltingly from her lips. 'The rabid dog...that night at the bungalow...it jumped up at you. Did it bite you? Scratch you? Touch you *at all*?'

The very same questions which Luke had thrown at her, and which at the time she had not understood. They trailed to a halt through trembling lips. She had heard, somewhere, that it took some time for rabies to develop. Was that where the shadow pointed?

'Luke, *please*. Tell me...'

'Dee, darling.'

For answer, Luke folded her in his arms, and shock added to the anguish and threatened Dee's reeling senses. Desperately she hung on to consciousness, willing Luke to answer her. Dreading what his answer might be.

'*Please*, Luke. I have to know.'

'The dog missed me by a yard. It was too weak to get anywhere near me.'

'Are you sure? You're not just saying that to...?'

He shook her gently. 'Dee, stop it! Stop torturing yourself. I'm telling you the honest truth. The dog got nowhere near me. Do you think I would ask you to marry me if I thought there was the slightest risk of my developing rabies?'

'M-marry you?' Sudden strength flowed back into Dee's failing limbs, but doubt still showed in her uplifted face. 'But...what about Mari?'

'What about Oliver?' he countered.

'Oliver's my brother.'

'Mari's my sister.'

Comprehension dawned, and laughter rocked them. Relieved laughter. Healing laughter, mingled with tears. They clung together until the storm passed, and when Dee had recovered sufficiently to be able to speak she gasped, 'I thought the stand erector explained about Oliver. I heard him say——'

'He didn't have time to finish. The stand started to tip, and we had to rescue it quickly. And afterwards there was no time, and I was in torment, not knowing. But I thought you knew about Mari. Kate said she had to leave some of her unmentionables in your room.'

'Kate told me about the unmentionables. She didn't explain who they belonged to.'

'I was madly jealous about Oliver. Will you forgive me? It made me bad-tempered, and I was a beast to you.'

'I was madly jealous about Mari.'

Forgiveness was unbelievably sweet, to give and to receive, and it was some time before Dee's lips were free to confess, 'I thought you were angry with me, about the newspaper photograph. That I might have tried to compromise you in front of the camera, to...' She stopped, her colour rising.

'It was the other way about. I thought if you saw a picture of us together you would realise what a perfect couple we make.'

'Do we?' innocently.

'You little minx!' Luke punished her suitably for tormenting him. 'What fools we've been,' he mourned, 'to waste so much precious time.'

His kisses made up for the loss. They explored her eager lips with tender care, rejoicing in their willing response, that had been so unwilling before. They traced an ardent line along the slender column of her throat to the sweetly perfumed, throbbing hollow at its base, and Luke groaned his pleasure as Dee buried her face in the fiery thickness of his hair, which muffled her admission, 'I must have loved you all along, and didn't know it.'

'I loved you from the very first moment I set eyes on you, in the foyer of your hotel.'

'I was hot, and sticky, and crumpled.'

'No other woman in the room could hold a candle to you. After I left you I went straight to Gita to angle an invitation for us both to go to dinner that night, so that she could find out for me if you were already engaged. You said you hadn't got a boyfriend with you, but I didn't know if you might have left one behind in England.'

'Gita did ask me,' Dee remembered.

'And you told her that you didn't intend to get married at all. That you were all set to be a career girl. I was in despair. I didn't know how to make you change your mind.'

'You didn't waste any time,' Dee accused him with a forgiving smile. 'You took complete control, of my job and me.' His masterful behaviour no longer had the power to infuriate.

'I felt desperately afraid when I knew you would be carrying the gems yourself.'

'I knew the risks, Luke. I've been trained to cope with them. Bill isn't as uncaring of his

couriers as you seem to think.' In the midst of
her happiness, loyalty made Dee defend her boss.

'I know that. I knew it all along. If it had been
any other woman I wouldn't have questioned the
matter. But love turned me into a coward, for
your sake. And you must admit,' he confessed
somewhat shamefacedly, 'it made a good excuse
to persuade Gita to invite you to go to the hill
station with them, where I could be sure of
joining you later. Those business meetings in
Calcutta seemed to go on forever,' he groaned at
the memory of their enforced separation.

'You're a devious, scheming——'

'I'm all of those things. But it worked.' His
kisses measured his satisfaction at the success of
his scheming, and a long, sweet silence ensued
until he told her, 'Mother and Dad will be home
soon, and Mari. I'm longing for them to meet
you. They'll love you.'

'There's going to be a christening soon in the
college chapel at home. You'll meet all of my
family then, all at once. Including my brand-new
nephew.'

In the turmoil of events which followed her
brother's call—was it only that morning?—Dee
had actually forgotten the momentous event to
which she had looked forward for so long, news
of which had reached her mere minutes before
they had set out for the cricket match.

'I hope they approve your choice.'

Luke looked uncharacteristically doubtful, and Dee was quick to reassure him, 'They'll love you too.' She grinned suddenly. 'Mother will approve. She's been trying to change my mind about getting married for ages. She's just like Gita. She thinks all women are made for marriage.'

'Maid for marriage.'

Luke's tongue twisted the word round, and gave it a new meaning, while his lips tenderly sealed the bond between them, and Dee answered in kind, easily fluent now in the language that had no words, because no words were necessary between them.

He paused long enough to ask, 'When will you marry me, Dee? Make it soon,' he begged.

'We're not even engaged yet.' She couldn't resist a little gentle teasing.

'I've got the ring.' He fumbled in his pocket, and slipped the ring on to her finger. 'I know it fits, because I tried it on in the bank in Delhi, just to make sure. You said you liked this one?' His eyes questioned her anxiously.

'Oh, yes, I do. It's the one we both liked.'

'I've been carrying it about in my pocket for days, trying to get you on your own.'

And she had been avoiding him, avoiding the happiness that could have been hers days ago. But that was behind her now, behind them both, and the future stretched ahead, as golden as the carpet of leaves on which they stood.

Luke lifted her hand and pressed his lips to the token of his love, and Dee said softly, 'It's lovely, Luke.'

'It can't compare with you. Nothing can.'

He folded her to him, and long, precious moments passed, oblivious of time, that brought the children creeping back to peep round the beech trees, wondering what had kept them for so long.

A mischievously smiling Gita rounded up her offspring, and hurried them away, and at long last Luke raised his head and remembered, 'You didn't tell me about Oliver's bet.'

Laughing, Dee told him, and added a contented, 'Oliver's won. I owe him a coffee.'

'No, he hasn't. I've won,' Luke contradicted, and lowered his lips to claim their prize.

**Fifty red-blooded, white-hot, true-blue hunks
from every State in the Union!**

Look for MEN MADE IN AMERICA! Written by some
of our most poplar authors, these stories feature fifty of
the strongest, sexiest men, each from a different state in
the union!

Two titles available every other month at your favorite
retail outlet.

In November, look for:

STRAIGHT FROM THE HEART by Barbara Delinsky
(Connecticut)
AUTHOR'S CHOICE by Elizabeth August (Delaware)

In January, look for:

DREAM COME TRUE by Ann Major (Florida)
WAY OF THE WILLOW by Linda Shaw (Georgia)

You won't be able to resist MEN MADE IN AMERICA!

Make Christmas a truly
Romantic experience—with

HARLEQUIN ROMANCE®

Wouldn't *you* love to kiss a tall, dark
Texan under the mistletoe? Gwen does,
in HOME FOR CHRISTMAS by
Ellen James. Share the experience!

Wouldn't *you* love to kiss a sexy
New Englander on a snowy Christmas
morning? Angela does, in Shannon
Waverly's CHRISTMAS ANGEL.
Share the experience!

Look for both of these Christmas
Romance titles, available in December
wherever Harlequin Books are sold.

(And don't forget that Romance novels
make great gifts! Easy to buy, easy to
wrap and just the right size for a
stocking stuffer. And they make a
wonderful treat when you need a break
from Christmas shopping, Christmas
wrapping and stuffing stockings!)

Harlequin is proud to present our best authors and their best books. Always the best for your reading pleasure!

Throughout 1993, Harlequin will bring you exciting books by some of the top names in contemporary romance!

In November, look for

BARBARA
DELINSKY

First, Best and Only

Their passion burned even stronger....

CEO Marni Lange didn't have time for nonsense like photographs. The promotion department, however, insisted she was the perfect cover model for the launch of their new career-woman magazine. She couldn't argue with her own department. She should have.

The photographer was a man she'd prayed never to see again. Brian Webster had been her first—and best—lover. This time, could she play with fire without being burned?

Don't miss FIRST, BEST AND ONLY by Barbara Delinsky... wherever Harlequin books are sold.

1993 Keepsake

CHRISTMAS

Stories

Capture the spirit and romance of Christmas with KEEPSAKE CHRISTMAS STORIES, a collection of three stories by favorite historical authors. The perfect Christmas gift!

Don't miss these heartwarming stories, available in November wherever Harlequin books are sold:

ONCE UPON A CHRISTMAS by Curtiss Ann Matlock
A FAIRYTALE SEASON by Marianne Willman
TIDINGS OF JOY by Victoria Pade

ADD A TOUCH OF ROMANCE TO YOUR HOLIDAY SEASON WITH KEEPSAKE CHRISTMAS STORIES!

HX93

When the only time you have for yourself is...

Christmas is such a busy time—with shopping, decorating, writing cards, trimming trees, wrapping gifts....

When you do have a few *stolen moments* to call your own, treat yourself to a brand-new *short* novel. Relax with one of our Stocking Stuffers— or with all six!

Each STOLEN MOMENTS title
is a complete and original contemporary romance that's the perfect length for the busy woman of the nineties! Especially at Christmas...

And they make perfect **stocking stuffers**, too! (For your mother, grandmother, daughters, friends, co-workers, neighbors, aunts, cousins—all the other women in your life!)

Look for the STOLEN MOMENTS display in December

STOCKING STUFFERS:

HIS MISTRESS Carrie Alexander
DANIEL'S DECEPTION Marie DeWitt
SNOW ANGEL Isolde Evans
THE FAMILY MAN Danielle Kelly
THE LONE WOLF Ellen Rogers
MONTANA CHRISTMAS Lynn Russell

HSM2

 WORLDWIDE LIBRARY